Adventures of a Jackeroo AND OTHER TALES...

Written and Illustrated by

Steve McGregor

STEVE MCGREGOR BOOKS

ISBN 978-0-6453543-1-7

SECOND EDITION

Dedicated to Phil Thompson of Enngonia
and all the Bushies I have met along the way

Index

The Bruce from Bondi Story

FORWARD

To the city slicker sitting in their favourite chair by their fans and sipping a cool drink; the life of those dwelling in the countryside are worlds apart.

Many of those who live close to the sea, as do a major portion of Australia's population, promise themselves that one day they will take a visit to the Australian countryside and somehow never get around to it. The closest they may get is to hang a nicely framed picture on the wall with gum trees and a few sheep busily cropping the straw coloured grass.

It is therefore, refreshing to read this book "Adventures of a Jackeroo" and have a laugh or two at the hapless hero, Bruce. It is an introduction to country life in a small way and may encourage some readers to venture forth and take a drive out to the Aussie bush and spend a few days enjoying another world. You see this book is set in the 1950's when life out west in the state of New South Wales was more basic than it is today.

For a young boy like Bruce, born and bred in Bondi close by the famous beach, traveling to Enngonia, near Bourke, and training to be a Jackeroo (trainee property manager) was a very brave thing to do. However, as Bruce said he would do anything to avoid school work and we can't blame him for that can we?

The escapades of our doubtful hero are amusing and in fact may remind us of our own efforts to adjust to adult life and in doing so trying to make as few mistakes as possible. For the younger readers of this book the illustrations may also provide some fun and show how Bruce from Bondi lived, for a few short years in the dry countryside of Booleroo Sheep Station far from home.

CAST OF CHARACTERS

Bob the Brumby - Old Iron Mouth one of the stock horses

Bruce from Bondi - a young Australian boy who leaves home to become a Jackeroo

Big Phil - Bruce's father, Phil Thompson

Blackie - the Foreman

Bludger - a drover

Bluey - another Jackeroo, a real dope

Booleroo Sheep Station - sometimes spelt Boolaroo Bruce's place of employment

Cheryl - The Boss' daughter

Constable Murphy - or Plod the local policeman

Flossy the Mare - a gentle horse for beginners

Greta - the Alsatian dog owned by Bruce's love, Jane.

Jackie - the aborigine who goes walkabout and also is a good tracker

Jane - Bruce's girl friend, her father owns a Pub.

Jacko - the fearsome brute of a cook from Engonnia later to be employed at Booleroo

Lilly - beautiful blond friend of Cheryl from Sydney

Madam Troubridge - the lady hairdresser

Mary - Bruce's Mum, Mary Thompson

Mrs. Fisher - The Boss' wife or missus

Mrs. Gobbers - a neighbour somewhere on the Party line telephone

O'Flaherty - the owner of the mad cow.

Pommie Drover - the would be hero

Rancid - the ram that refuses to be caught and cleaned up. He is a real stinker.

Rusty - another Jackeroo from the Boolaroo station

Razza - a Drover

Ralph - the handsome batsman from Enngonia

Sally the Sow - Sally the giant pet pig

Spot, alias Spottie - a fox terrier, house dog who loves Bruce

Shanahan - the Butcher

Skeeter - one of the Drovers

The Boss - Mr Fisher the owner of Boolaroo Sheep Station

Wendel "Whippy" Whippet - Bruce's mate

BRUCE - starts off as a real smart alec however, country life has a way of smoothing out the bumps when he became a Jackeroo. Eventually he finds love and then a job at a Bondi Beach Hotel. What more could he want?

BLUEY - makes Bruce look like a genius. In Australia usually anyone who is a red hair is called Bluey. Don't ask me why. Bluey eventually left Booleroo after becoming lost one night in the paddock he found that country life was not for him. He works in a fish shop just around the corner from Bruce. He should keep his mouth closed because the flies will cause a few problems.

WHIPPY the Drover and head Roustabout – a sensible mentor to Bruce who really needed guidance. Whippy became head man at Booleroo and eventually married Cheryl, Mr. Fisher's daughter.

JACKIE - is the local aboriginal tracker and manages to get some work and then goes walkabout. However upon his return to Booleroo he was called in to track down whomever or whatever was eating the flowers in Mrs Fisher's garden. We think that Jackie was pulling everyone's leg.

SKEETER A little fellow always quick to give his opinions who was one of the drovers working with Bruce - In Australia if you are called Skeeter then you are usually a small person, a Mosquito of a man, hence Skeeter, you know "Mosskeeter".

SPOT The Fox Terrier House dog who loved Bruce, sometimes called Spottie. A good kisser and a great friend.

JACKO the giant cook who managed to frighten everyone he meets.

MADAME TROUBRIDGE who eventually escaped from the outhouse when Sally the Sow was apprehended.

THE BOYS IN THE CRICKET TEAM Bruce's workmates and some of the Engonnia fellows are a great bunch.

CHAPTER 1

Bruce from Bondi

Bruce had decided that being a student at school was boring being cooped up in a class room sitting there tuning out as the teacher droned on.

He had perfected the steady look of concentration, and with his pen poised over a clipboard as if ready to take notes always seemed to lull the teacher into believing that Bruce was paying close attention.

At the end of the year Bruce at last prevailed on his ever suffering parents that he was wasted at school and was meant for better things.

"Oh, Bruce what will you do?" wailed his mother when he told them of his decision to leave school.

"Yeh, son you need an education, something that I didn't have and I was hoping that you would stick with it and go to university or at least get a trade. You know when I was young, young fellas would get an apprenticeship" ... droned his father.

Bruce all this time was sitting there with a serious look on his face and was of course thinking of other things, you see he had perfected that look. In fact he had years of practice. I guess you could call Bruce a know all. In other parts of Bondi he would be called a smart aleck.

Bruce, had enough. He held up his hand as if to stop his parents from any more talk and announced, "I'm gunna be a Jackeroo."

"A Jackeroo" his parents echoed in amazement, "you have never been to the country let alone mentioned that you were interested."

"Yep, I've been thinkin' for some time now and learning to manage a sheep property appeals to me" Bruce said "and also I was speaking with Mr. Whippet down at the Pub ...." and he said ....

"Down at the Pub!" his parents yelled in unison.

"Oh, come on, I was jest walkin' along and this geezer was sitting outside with a few of his old mates talkin' and drinkin' a few beers and ...."

"But you don't even know this man do you?" said his mother.

"Nah, not really, but I got to talking with him and he, er, Mr. Whippet, said that he was down from Bourke for a bit of R& R and they were always lookin' fer a Jackeroo...."

"R &R wot's that?" said Dad

"It means rest and recreation that's what," said Bruce with a knowing smile.

(Yes, Bruce was a smart aleck alright.)

"Well," said his father with an angry look in his eye.

"Oh, Dad let me go and see the world. It will make a man of me," said Bruce.

"Yes it will, dear," said Bruce's Mum to her husband who was standing there breathing heavily.

"Bruce may do well and it may help, it surely can't do any harm."

At that Bruce knew he had succeeded and school was finished as far as he was concerned.

"Whacko the diddly oh," thought Bruce.

He rushed out of the room with a whoop and a holler and scampered off to the Pub to tell his new mate Wendel Whippet the good news that he would be joining him as a Jackaroo.

"That job will be a goodun for yer at Bourke mate and I will send yuz a letter with all the details."

"Common Whippy there is a beer for you," called one of his mates.

One thing about the Australian country boys they could be men of their word. Some weeks went by and Bruce was just about to give up and think that his school holidays would never end when a letter came for him from Whippy in the post.

Speedily Bruce tore open the envelope and sure enough Whippy had teed up a job for him at Booleroo at Bourke, a property along the Colerina Road from North Bourke. His job would be mustering sheep and learning all about sheep and shearing and all the things that were necessary on a property in Australia out the back of beyond in the 1950's.

Bruce was pretty excited and packed a bag with some clothes to catch the bus to the Central railway station for his long trip up the country to Nyngan and beyond.

"Hooroo Mum and Bye dad," called Bruce.

His parents stood together on the veranda in the early morning light with the magpies carolling in the surrounding trees and waved as their son walked out of sight around the corner.

"Oh, Phil I will miss him so, poor boy who will look after him, I just cannot bear to think."

By this time Big Phil had gotten used to the idea of having his son out of the house and had a glimmer of an idea that Bruce may benefit from a bit of toughening up. He sure could use it.

"Hopefully he will learn a lot Mary and when he comes home one day he will be a man and have matured. That will only be for the best."

Later that morning Bruce arrived at Central Railway Station and made his way to the ticket office and bought a one way ticket to Nyngan. He thanked the man in jail behind the bars and sauntered off to the platform to climb aboard his train. The steam engine was puffing away and the humph whumpf of its breath thrilled young Bruce.

"Jeez, what an adventure. Gosh this is better than being stuck in a classroom being bored to death."

Bruce looked at the ticket in his hand and eventually found his way to the Second Class carriages where he opened the door to his "dog box" and shoved his bag inside and climbed up the steps and found himself in the box. The small carriage consisted of two benches facing each other and with another door to the corridor of the train.

He shoved his bag under his seat and looked out the window at the people scurrying along the platform all hurrying to get on the train.

After what seemed like a very long time whistles were heard and shouting of all aboard and the train banged and bucked as it started to gather speed and move off from the station.

Bruce looked out and marvelled at the sight of the platform starting to drop away quite quickly and especially laughed when he saw a fat gentleman come running along waving his arms.

“Jeez, he has missed the train poor blighter,” said Bruce and laughed as he gave him a wave.

The day was just starting for the big city and it took awhile for the train to steam on out of the suburbs and eventually the houses became fewer and trees and grasslands were the main scenery outside Bruce’s window.

Bruce amused himself by looking at his fellow passengers and eventually became sick of that and dozed and dreamed about the fun he would have at Bourke.

Towards late afternoon Bruce found himself on the station at Nyngan in the west of New South Wales a country that he was soon to get to know quite well.

Bruce looked around and found his way to the Hotel in Nyngan where he was to meet Whippy outside. Whippy was driving down from Booleroo Sheep Station and take him back to his new home. The train only went as far as Nyngan and the straight as a die road; the Mitchell Highway, would take him the 120 miles or so to Bourke and then out another 50 miles Nor East to Booleroo Sheep Station.

“Now where is Whippy?” said Bruce, “Jeez I’ve been waiting for an hour and no show. I hope he hasn’t forgotten.”

“Oye, Bruce, over here.”

Bruce looked around and with a feeling of relief he espied his new friend Mr. Wendel Whippet leaning out of the cabin of a rusty old truck with a few hay bales on the tray behind it.

“Gidday mate glad to see yer,” said Bruce.

“Hello and climb aboard Bruce and we’ll be off mate. We have to get to Booleroo before its too dark coz I don’t like driving at night. The Roos are fierce and thick as fleas on a blanket at present.”

“Gosh, what do you mean fierce?” said Bruce?

“Oh, wot I mean is that there are lots of ‘em and they have a bad habit of jumpin' in front of your truck and kersplash and kerbang," said Whippy as he rolled his eyes.

"Yeh, hitting a big roo at 40 miles an hour is pretty rough mate and can do a lot of damage to the truck. Yer sure don't want one of them biguns come through the windscreen at yer and end up in your lap. "Yes, they will give yer a big kickin', that's for sure."

"Jeez they must be big, if they do that much damage" said Bruce imagining giant kangaroos whizzing all around him in the night.

CHAPTER 2

Rancid the Ram

Hours later the truck turned off and after driving over the final cattle grid and in a cloud of dust passed the property's grand gates with the Booleroo Sheep Station sign over them.

“It will only be a mile or so now Bruce until we get there,” said Whippy over the noise of the roaring engine.

“I will introduce yer to the boss mate,” ...... and we can then take you down to the shearer's quarters where the other blokes are and I can then introduce yer to Mister Fisher.”

They eventually stopped in front of a low bungalow, in clouds of more dust and mounted the steps up to the veranda. “Better wipe yer feet mate.”

“Hello Bruce glad you could make it and welcome to Booleroo Station. I will leave you to Whippy and he can make you feel at home. You won't see much of me because the foreman will be giving you a steer around here and you will learn a lot from him and Whippy.”

“Thanks Mistah Fisha,” said Bruce shaking the Boss's hand and he escaped from what felt like and interview with his old headmaster at the school hundreds of miles to the south and far from his thoughts for ever more.

“C'mon Bruce here we are, home sweet home,” said Whippy as they drove up in front of the shearers quarters.

A group of men were sitting outside before a small fire and a dark fellow, who looked like an aborigine was strumming a guitar and singing a song with a nasal singing voice. The men were smoking and talking amongst themselves and all stopped when Whippy walked up with Bruce.

“Hey fellas this a new chum just up from Sydney, say hello to Bruce.”

“Hello Bruce,” came the chorus.

After a few hellos back Bruce sat on the steps of the shearer's hut and after awhile the fellows decided to call it a night and slipped away from the fire to their bunks. They had as usual; a very early start the next morning to get out and do their work.

Whippy led Bruce to an empty bunk and left him to it.

Bruce by this time was reeling with exhaustion, because he had not slept too well the night before as he was so excited and was soon dead to the world.

The next thing he knew was a loud banging sound and the foreman was going around waking everybody up by banging on an empty kerosene tin.

"Rise and shine boys, cooks got the brekkie ready for us and a hot cuppa, so get movin', came the call."

Bruce copied what the other fellows were doing and soon found himself sitting with the other chaps wolfing down toast and baked beans and washing it all down with mugs of sweet white tea.

"Now your job today Bruce is to get Booleroo's pet ram, called Rancid, and tie a line on 'im and bring him up to the shearing shed so we can clip 'im," said the foreman.

Now all this talk was kind of foreign to Bruce but he was eager and he got up from the table and followed Whippy outside to look for Rancid.

"I don't know what I am looking for but Rancid is a funny name for a sheep," said Bruce.

"Yeh, it's 'cause he stinks," said one of the jackeroos as he strolled past.

Whippy pointed with his chin to a speck of gray matter way down the end of the paddock. "There is Rancid Bruce. Here is some rope and you can walk on down and collar 'im and bring 'im back up, mate?"

"Why does Rancid stink, Whippy?" asked Bruce.

"Well he hasn't been sheared for a few years coz we can't catch him and he has a few layers of dags and things," was the casual reply.

If Bruce was a more experienced sheepman, he would have known that there was a reason for the non capture and shearing of Rancid, but he was soon to find out.

Bruce set off down the paddock. It was only early but already the sun was hot, in fact it was bloody hot and getting hotter as Bruce walked down to Rancid.

"Funny the more I walk towards the thing the further away he seems to get," said Bruce to himself. "I will just walk faster."

Bruce eventually realised that the sheep was slowly drifting away the closer he got and he never noticed until he would look up again and Rancid would be that much further away.

Eventually after what was a very long time, Bruce got closer to the animal which seemed to be getting tired of the encroaching human nuisance.

The closer he got to the beast the bigger Bruce realised it was. In fact it was huge. The Ram for that is what it was seemed to be burdened by years of uncut fleece, burs, dags and more dags. In fact the thing stank to high heaven.

"Phew, I don't know if I am going to enjoy grabbing that thing. I wonder of it bites," muttered Bruce as he swiped at a few million flies.

The Ram stopped and gazed at Bruce. Bruce stopped and gazed right back. He noticed that the Ram had light eyes that looked fierce but Whippy said that Rams don't bite. And Bruce believed his mate Whippy.

Mind you Whippy omitted to mention one thing about Rancid apart from its disgusting stench. And that was Rancid would charge and butt him.

Usually shearers would handle such behaviour with ease for the sheep were not that strong but in the case of old Rancid; well he was huge and strong and heavy. He was used to being his own boss and was in no hurry to be led up to the shearing sheds and be shorn of anything.

"C'mon Rancid, there's a good fellow, come on over to Brucie and I will tie youse up and we will fix yer up and ....."

Rancid gazed at the human who was standing there waving at him. Now what was the stupid human doing wondered Rancid. Is he trying to provoke me? If he is then he is doing a very good job of it. (Author's note: Now that is how I would have imagined a Ram would think or something close to it)

Rancid put his head down and charged

Suddenly Rancid moved, in fact he moved like greased lightening and was just a blur and he was charging, with his head down straight for Bruce.

"Oh, Gawd he's gunna hit me," was the fleeting thought which came to Bruce's mind and he didn't even have time to run.

Crash!

Bruce went down in the dust and lay there stunned. "Jeez I've been hit by a truck," thought Bruce.

Rancid gave a self satisfied "Baaa" and trotted off a few yards and stood there waiting to see if the silly human wanted more of the butting that was the Ram's entertainment.

Bruce, got to his feet and looked around for Rancid but he was looking in the wrong direction and suddenly got a whiff of some God awful stench and Bang, it was too late. Down he went again.

"Bugger you Rancid. I will leave yerz to it you rotten bloody awful stinkin' daggy looking wreck of a thing," screamed Bruce by now red in the face as he waved off a few more thousand flies.

Bruce clambered to his feet and ran about twenty yards and stopped and looked over his shoulder at Rancid who stood there placidly nuzzling at some dry grass. Bruce shook his fist at the Ram and left him to it.

He walked on back to the sheds to report that his first job at the property was a failure; the bloody Ram was too much of a handful for him.

"Jeez how am I goin' to explain this one, I am off to a pretty bad start I reckon, "grizzled Bruce.

Eventually Bruce arrived back at the shearer's shed and quickly guzzled down some water from a canvas water bags swinging in the shade.

"Boy is it hot. It's a bit different from being down at Bondi. It would be a lot cooler there and I wonder of I could get a job there as a life guard. I could save good lookin' sheilas and help them eat their ice creams and things," thought Bruce.

"Boy it's hot!"

"Oh, there you are Bruce how did you get on with Rancid the Ram mate?" said Whippy with a big grin.

Bruce looked up and noticed that not only was his friend there but every other shearer was hanging out of a window or door to see if he had done any good in bringing back Rancid.

"No luck Whippy I'm afraid I couldn't grab the bastard," said Bruce.

"Look over there you've done good mate,"

Sure enough when Bruce swung around to look where Whippy was pointing, guess who was standing there with a silly look on his big sheep face?

Rancid of course.

The stinking horrible looking thing was standing almost right behind him and gazing at him placidly through the fence.

"The bloody thing has followed you home," laughed Whippy and all the boys guffawed and shook their heads and had a good giggle at the expense of Bruce.

Bruce looked over at the Ram.

"Baa," said Rancid.

"I'll Baa you" ... grumbled Bruce, "If I hadda a gun I woulda shot ya," said Bruce.

Rancid just looked at him with those crazy sheep's eyes and gave a burp and emitted a quiet Baa.

"Bondi is looking really good at the moment," thought Bruce. "Now how am I gunna tell Mum and Dad I am goin' to be a life saver?"

"I will thinka something."

CHAPTER 3

Bob the Brumby

"Jeez it's hot", said Bruce as he swiped at a few flies looking for a drink.

It was over 100 in the shade out there at Booleroo in New South Wales' west and up near the Queensland border was especially hot, or it felt like it to the new chum Bruce from Bondi.

Bruce had been a reluctant student at school, he knew he was meant for better things and sitting in the classroom while various teachers droned on was not for him.

Consequently, Bruce had announced to his ever suffering parents that he was off to seek new horizons and adventure. Imagine their surprise when he told them he was going to be a Jackeroo.

The result of Bruce's career shift was seeing him now astride a stock horse sitting under a tree giving sparse shade as he looked around searching for some errant ewes secreted in the scrub and lignum that covered the paddocks which in this part of the country stretched for miles.

"Jeez it's hot," said Bruce.

Bruce sat there and drifted off daydreaming. He imagined cool water. The surf of Bondi. Ice Creams and lovely young two piece costumed girls with ice cream complexions. With ice cream like cool touch to his fevered brow. Ah ice cream!

He came out of his day dream and swiped at a few more flies.

"Jeez the flies are driving me crazy I don't know how I am putting up with this. I will never get used to the heat and the dust and the flies and the stupid sheep and ....", he rambled on.

His horse shifted under him and again Bruce came back from Bondi where he was imagining himself diving through a clear green wave as the sand of the ocean's floor drifted below him.

"Hell, this will not do!" exclaimed Bruce

He turned the very tame old mare and headed back to the shearers quarters where he had his bunk.

"I will just tell the foreman that I couldn't find 'em, that should do it and I can then put my head in the horse trough and keep it there for as long as I can hold my breath," so he thought about cool things and ignored the flies as the crows arked forlornly above him in the trees.

Some three months ago when Bruce arrived at Booleroo Sheep Station out on the Colerina Road at Bourke, Bruce had found that he had to learn fast, in fact real fast.

The foreman came to see him and said, Bruce, "The first thing you hafta do is learn to ride a horse. Can you ride by the way?"

"No, sir," said Bruce, "but I am willing to have a crack at it."

"Well take old Flossy the mare over there, as he pointed to a horse sleeping in the shade of the hut."

"OK sir, when do I start?"

"Now of course so go and get a saddle and a horse blanket and meet me out here as soon as you can. It's real hot and I have to get off in the truck to Bourke to the general store for some provisions."

Bruce saddled up and climbed aboard. His feet stuck out a bit but he seemed to be doing alright except when Flossy shambled into a trot Bruce found that he rolled around a lot and jiggled up and down until one would think he was agreeing with crowds of people. In fact at one stage he almost bit his tongue.

"Jeez, it is a long way up here and I hope I don't fall off," said our hero with clacking teeth.

Bruce improved during the day and it was not until the end of the week did Mr. Fisher the boss come over to him.

Looking up Mr. Fisher said, "If you don't mind Bruce hop down and give me the reins for old Flossy, my grandson is up from Dubbo visiting and I would like him to have a safe ride while he is here."

"Alright boss," said Bruce, "but what will I do now because the foreman has asked me to gather up a few strays out in the south paddock."

Mr. Fisher thought for a bit and said, "Take Bob the Brumby he is alright as a ride and he will not buck you off. You should be alright. There are a lot of Roos down there but the stock are hard to find because of the lignum scrub."

Bruce went down to the horse enclosure and managed to find Bob and eventually with a lot of puffing and grumbling got a saddle on him.

"Alright Bob, me boy, Giddyup."

Bob trotted off and Bruce was rather pleased with himself.

"Jeez it's hot," said Bruce as he looked around him as he ambled along, "I cannot see any strays around here. Whippy says that you would not think it would be hard but they seemed to know when shearing is on and shoot through."

At last Bruce saw a few dirty looking ewes in the scrub and pulled the reins to signal Bob that he should go left.

To Bruce's surprise Bob kept on going. In fact try as he might Bruce could neither steer the horse or make it stop.

"Jeez Bob you have a mind of yer own that's for sure. Whoa, stop, there's a good fella, oh come on Bobbie, mate," said Bruce plaintively.

Try as he might Bruce could not get the horse to stop

Bruce was in a fix. Bob the Brumby would not buck that was true but he could not be directed or stopped in fact Bruce was a prisoner on the animals back.

Bob ambled along most of the morning all in one direction and despite all his efforts and entreaties, Bruce could not do a thing with him. About midday the two figures in the barren landscape arrived at a dam or as Whippy called them "tanks".

Bob the Brumby shambled into a trot and then a canter, mind you a gallop was asking too much, and Bruce almost thought they were going to take a header into the muddy water.

Bob drew up in a cloud of dust, shook himself whinnied half heartedly and lowered his head and had a long drink, with much grunting and guzzling sounds.

Bruce almost fell off but was determined to stay where he was.

"Jeez Bob, haven't you had enough? There is no way I am going to get off yah until I get you back home. I don't want to be left out here in the dark."

Bob finished his drink and turned around and headed off in another direction with the forlorn figure of a very hot and sunburned Bruce perched on his back, waving like a windmill to keep the flies away.

Hours went by and the day clouded over and in fact it started to rain. Just a steady drizzle really but Bruce was miserable. He now found that he hated horses and especially Bob the Brumby.

More time went by and just up ahead Bruce saw a figure standing there with his dog beside the track.

"Jeez if it isn't the foreman," thought Bruce. "I hope I am not going to get into trouble."

"Gidday boss," said Bruce.

"Good evening Bruce, just where have you been mate?"

That is when Bruce started. He spoke without taking a breath for minutes at a time explaining about the dang, dratted, blankety blank iron mouthed stooge of a horse and blamed his lost day on the horse.

In fact Bruce explained how the horse would not stop and he tried to steer him but had no luck.

The foreman held up his hand, “Yes Bruce, old Bob is known for having a mind of his own but he didn’t buck you off did he?”

“No, but er ....”

“Don’t worry Bruce go up ahead and take his gear off and give him a rub down and a mouthful of oats. He should be OK if you lead him into a stall, there will be hay there and the old fellow’s most probably tired.”

Bruce went off grumbling. “Tired, the old fellow is most probably tired, I am gunna get outta here, I am gunna get back to the beach and I will never be in the country again. I am not meant for this life and it’s just not fair.”

“I will tell ‘em tomorrow that my Mum is sick and I have to go home. That should do the trick.”

“Boy am I looking forward to getting back to Bondi. I can be a life guard and I can ....”

Bruce ambled off and his figure faded into the darkness.

All that was heard in the darkness was a sarcastic little 'neigh’ from Bob the Brumby.

“Jeez it’s hot”.

CHAPTER 4

Country Race Meeting

It was a hot and cloudless sky one Saturday afternoon in the country town of Enngonia and Bruce the Jackeroo, up from Bondi, was standing in the public bar surrounded by his fellow Jackeroos from Booleroo Sheep Station.

"Hurry up Bruce will ya, just finish that beer and c'mon with us over to the race track the races will be over before you are finished," griped Whippy.

Bruce had a lemon squash in front of him but beside that was his beer. Anyone over twenty-one years of age was allowed a beer in Aussie pubs but Bruce had only seventeen summers under his belt so the publican allowed him into his establishment but only on the understanding that Bruce did not imbibe, as he would say.

He was always careful that the local plod, Constable Murphy, would espy an underage drinker and his hotel could be closed for a day as punishment.

Bruce quickly downed his beer and left the squash behind as he exited through the swinging bats ears doors to the street.

He was immediately hit by the glare of the day and hastily shoved his broad brimmed hat on his head and peered out at the sun blasted world of Enngonia's main street.

"C'mon all you guys, hurry up, we have five minutes before the next race starts," yelled an oaf waving a schooner as he ran past.

"Oh c'mon Bruce your sweetheart Lilly is waiting for you," smirked Rusty.

Bruce blushed and shuffled his feet but said nothing as he quickly got into top gear and caught up with his mates who were reeling down the street.

"Jeez, Rusty, I reckon the boys are a little worse for wear, they should not have had so many beers," said Bruce.

“Oh that’s part of the fun mate,” said his pal digging him in the ribs with a laugh.

Races were not much fun for Bruce as he was not that keen on horses especially after the episode of being on Bob the Brumby, but that was another story, and one he would very much like to forget.

The best part of the races to young Bruce was having the opportunity of gazing on his love, Lilly, a blonde haired maiden who, being a friend of the bosses daughter was visiting Booleroo. However, Bruce had not yet had the chance to speak with her other than to stare moonily at her and say “Gidday ow are yerz?”

Now Bruce thought his time had come and he would go and look for her. To hell with looking at horse races.

The announcer’s voice came over the Tannoy, “Listen up everybody the fifth is gunna start so get yor bets in and don’t tell plod.”

The announcement was met with loud guffaws but a few of those present quickly looked around to see if plod, otherwise known as Constable Murphy was looming up anywhere. For some reason plod did not like them setting their bets with the local SP Bookie. Never mind that SP bookmaking was illegal. Who cared anyway at the ‘back of Bourke.’

In the meantime the fellows who were now decidedly the worse for wear from an excess of Tooheys amber brew had decided the proceedings needed a bit of livening up and so some wag convinced the local O’Flaherty to fetch his cow.

I will need some help boys, said O’Flaherty with a hiccup, and so a few of the boys went with the farmer to put a rope on O’Flaherty’s crazy cow and bring her back and see if they could enter her in a race.

Now this cow was no ordinary Friesian or Jersey she was a cross in more ways than one. Some of the guys down the pub reckon she was bred from a lion and a wild buffalo or something really bad and wicked because she was big and well muscled as well as having a fearsome temperament.

“She‘s been a bad bugger from the day she tottered to her feet or hooves when she was a little un,” said one of the wobbling Jackeroos.

“Where did she get them horns from?”

Bruce could see that O'Flaherty was getting into the swing of things and was quick to join in and see what his raging mad cow could do.

"She did not allow anyone to milk her and so her udders av been thin an empty like a empty football," said Whippy to Bruce.

"Old Moo Cow never thunk she wiz a cow and I dunno why I keep her. I am just a sentimental old fool," he hiccupped as he downed another Tooheys KB."

The boys were definitely out for some fun and it took seven of them all with a rope on her to drag her along to the race track. All this was going on with oaths from the boys as the cow pulled and charged every way but she could not get loose.

Mind you a few of the crowd noticed that the cow never made a moo or even a grunt she just stared and rolled her eyes at her tormenters and gave the impression that great carnage would take place if she ever got free.

"C'mon boys put a rope around her middle coz we gotta ride her in the fifth and ya never know we may win a race." Yelled one of the drunken louts who had joined the merry group of fellows from Booleroo.

The fifth race of the day was just about to start and the mangy mob of horses doubling as race horses were skittering around behind the starting line, amidst much shouting and waiving of arms by all the owners and jockeys.

"Let's put Bruce up on er, he will enjoy a good ride," whispered one of the Booleroo lads,

"Good idea chorused a few of the lads," with a cheer.

Suddenly Bruce found himself grabbed by a dozen pairs of hands and was swung into the air and hoisted up onto the broad back of the mad cow.

Bruce let out a yell and then a scream as the men and his ex-mates let go the last of the ropes that held her.

It was as if the bull had rushed into an arena and was circling the toreador. The mad cow was frothing at the mouth and making a loud grunting noise as she pawed the ground, as she realised there was something on her back that now demanded her attention.

“It’s hard to believe that there thing is a cow and not a bull,” said Rusty looking around for a place of safety.

Bruce hung onto the mad cow and screamed

With a bellow the cow took off.

“Boy can she run,” yelled Whippy.

“I tol’ ya so”, hiccupped O’Flaherty.

In no time old cow had joined the race alright but was equally determined to corkscrew her rider off.

The boys thought it was all a great joke and stopped their shouting to see the group of horses with all manner of riders clinging to their backs galloped closer.

Then a great cloud of dust enveloped all as Bruce and his trustee steed O’Flaherty’s Old Cow merged with the racing horses as they thundered past .

In no time chaos reigned as the stock horses, masquerading as racing horses, reverted to type and all skidded to a stop and started to muster the cow with Bruce clinging to her angry back.

The picture of seven stock horses rounding up a warlike cow and a white faced Bruce from Bondi perched precariously on her back was a new one for the sleepy town of Enngonia.

"Lookit Bruce he's enjoying himself, whatta guy," yelled Rusty clutching an empty beer bottle to his chest.

"Yeh, he's wavin' at us, friendly fella," drawled one of the boys.

"Wait a minute he's not, he's yelling out somethin'."

"Wot's he sayin'."

Faintly above the noise of drunken race goers, shouting jockeys and the stamping of scores of hooves a faint cry was heard.

"Help, get me orf her! Heeeeeeeeeelp!" Came the cry from brave Bruce the stand in jockey.

"Yeh, lads I don't think Bruce is joining in so good that lemon squash did not help him with his riding abilities. Now if he had a few Tooheys KB," laughed Whippy.

"C'mon lads let's go an help Bruce I don't think the fifth is gunna finish."

CHAPTER 5

Country Cricket Match

Bruce was heartily sick of country life. The flies and the dust plus the heat made a very bad mix as far as he was concerned and he very much regretted leaving the relative cool clime of Bondi to go and work as a Jackeroo on a sheep station up near Bourke.

Ralph the stock and station agent looked a picture of elegance

He was sitting on one of the stock horses, with one of his legs over the pommel, under the sparse shade of a tree and watching over his charges. The flies gave out a steady hum and the bush was quiet, not even a crow made a call.

The mob of sheep that Bruce was watching numbered over a hundred or so and Bruce's job was to muster them and work them on back to the sheep pens by the shearer's shed so they could be shorn.

"Phew, this heat is rotten, bloody flies!" grumbled our hero as he took off his broad brimmed hat and wiped his dripping forehead with the sleeve of his shirt.

"Jeez, I wonder how I can get out of doin' this, I could say that I was sick or I had a sore back or something and then they would let me do some light duties around the homestead," said Bruce.

"In fact working around the homestead really appeals coz the boss' daughter Cheryl, with the big shoulders, has brought a friend home from boarding school in Bowral. Jeez, she is a real corker," said Bruce with a glitter in his eye as he thought of the blond haired blue eyed vision that was Cheryl's best friend, Lilly.

There was a sound of the clopping of a horses hooves coming towards Bruce and he sat up straighter in the saddle as one of his mates came into sight.

"Hey there Bruce come on back now as we have to all go into town. Just leave the mob there and we can get them tomorrow," yelled Whippy one of his fellow companions.

"Jeez Whippy wots up what are we goin' to do in town?" asked Bruce.

"The Boss has a bet with one of his mates that the Booleroo Boys can beat his Engonnia boys in a cricket match. So we are all going to have a game and then a few beers."

The two Jackeroos then kicked their horses into a run and raced back to the shearer's quarters to get dressed in their fancy town clothes.

After a bumpy and noisy drive the Booleroo team drove up in a cloud of dust at the paddock near the Engonia Hotel.

Not many of the fellows in either the Booleroo or Enngonia teams had any cricket gear and except for a bat and a ball that was pretty well it.

The only one who had creams and pads was Ralph the clerk from the Stock and Station Agent in town who rather fancied himself as a sportsman and a batsman with an average of over 40.

He was not wanted by the Engonnia team so he was elected to be an honorary Booleroo Team member.

Sticks were found and hammered into the hard yellow clay of the paddock by another bit of wood and soon the paddock was echoing to the screams and yells from the players and spectators.

"Jeez those blackfellas are noisy," said Bruce to Rusty.

"They are not all Blackfellas mate. The Enngonia boys from around here are alright until they snitch a dozen bottles of Flag Ale and in no time the quiet crew of 'em are as noisy as a bunch of galas in a wheat field," yelled Rusty as he tried to make himself heard above the yells and cooees from the inebriated crowd.

The Booleroo captain won the toss and Ralph was the opening batsman.

Cheers rang out as Ralph smiling nonchalantly and looking resplendent in his creams sauntered out to the wicket to take his place. Ralph was a local favourite of the girls thereabouts and his fair hair and slim build set the girl's hearts a flutter.

All the girls and Ralph too thought he looked magnificent.

"Hit it Ralph!" went up the cry as one of the Enngonia boys pounded down the makeshift pitch to bowl a slow one.

Ralph took a swing and hit the ball straight into the weatherboard side of the Pub with a mighty Bang.

Cheering and loud laughs resounded and all present thought Ralph was doing rather well as in no time he had amassed a score of over 43.

The crowd stopped their shouting until one of the fieldsmen leaning up against the pub reckoned that the walls would stand up to a thousand cricket balls from the crowd of boozed up onlookers.

Meanwhile Ralph was swinging away and sending the balls this way and that and really making the fieldsmen run around like an ant's nest that has been stepped on.

Suddenly there was a hush from the crowd as the new bowler a giant figure strolled over the paddock to the crease.

"It's me turn," growled the burly cook Jacko from the Enngonia team as he rolled up his sleeves over beefy forearms.

Now Jacko was a mountain of a man. He was six feet five inches in his socks and with great slabs of muscle and wearing his green singlet from the local woodcutter's team.

"Not even the flies have the nerve to bother Jacko," said one wag to the laughter of his mates.

"Jeez Rusty getaload of Jacko willya, his arms are as thick as me thighs," exclaimed Bruce.

"Sure are mate and he has a nasty temper and all the boys around Bourke avoid Jacko when he has had a few beers aboard."

"Do ya think he's had a few already Jacko?"

"Bound to have had mate."

"Ralphie had better watch out I reckon then", said Bruce very glad he was not out there facing the giant from the Engonnia team.

Jacko paced off about 50 paces before he started his run. By this time everyone could see that Ralph was nervous and was trembling slightly.

The boys in the cricket team and Jacko who was a giant of a man and really mean

Poor Ralph he knew that he was in deep trouble. He was watching the new big bowler closely and the man's meaty hair covered arms looked powerful. He could tell that Jacko was dangerous.

Ralph gulped and wiped some perspiration from his forehead.

"No need to try too hard Jacko it's only a game," called Ralph hoping to slow the bull elephant which was shortly going to be charging.

Jacko just gave a mean gap toothed grin, pawed the ground like an angry bull, and let out a loud growl.

At the sound of the growl and the sight of Jacko pawing the ground unnerved the champion batsman of the Booleroo team.

Jacko had by this time lurched into motion and had put his head down and started his lumbering run towards the crease.

Ralph saw what appeared to be a locomotive headed for him at a thousand miles an hour and the sweat started to drip off him, he couldn't stop his trembling.

Jacko let go a mighty over-arm of a bowl and the red ball streaked towards the shaking Ralph, who by now wanted to be somewhere else.

In fact the unnerved Ralph turned his back on the ball, dropped his bat and started to run away.

"Bonk!" went the ball.

"Splat!" went Ralph as he hit the ground in another cloud of dust.

There was silence at the Enngonia paddock cricket match. All present froze and waited with bated breath to see if the hapless batsman would clamber to his feet.

"Jeez, I think Jacko has killed him," said Bruce.

After that pause of silence and when all had frozen, everybody started shouting again and some ran to the sprawled body of Ralph to see what the damage was.

"Jeez Rusty let's get over there and see what Jacko did to Ralphie, he mighta killed 'im."

"Yeh Bruce I heard that ball hit his head alright it was like another ball had hit the side of the pub."

“No need to make a joke of it mate this could be serious”, said the Foreman from Booleroo who happened to overhear the two Jackeroos.

As Bruce and Rusty ran out to the crowd which had now surrounded the still form of Ralph, a thousand thoughts flashed through Bruce’s head. You see for some time Bruce had rather imagined himself as a Doctor or a Vet.

He once read the Readers Digest when he was waiting for the dentist and the article; ‘I am Joe’s Prostate’ or whatever, really impressed him as to how easy it was to do operations.

Bruce considered he had a good grasp of the basics, such as; the problems of germs could easily be fixed by Dettol.

The stitching up by a good needle and some fishing line and ...

He could use a real sharp knife and adapt some wire coat hangers for opening up and a wire brush to give everything a good clean out then a good dose of Dettol.

The budding genius Dr Bruce administered to Ralph the downed batsman

Pain killers well that could be fixed by some Bex or Vincents APC.

Bruce pushed through the crowd and knelt by the elegant cream clad batsman lying still in the dust.

"Get some of the boys to hold him down," yelled Bruce who was chaffing at the bit to play doctor and taking over with a good deal of excitement.

"If he gets too frisky put a chaff bag on him and then sit on the chaff bag," instructed the budding surgeon, Dr. Bruce from Bondi.

Bruce thought he would try and wake up Ralph from his slumber and started patting him on the head.

Ralph started to come too and as through a haze opens his eyes and looks up to see the crowd standing over him and the dopey Jackeroo from Booleroo station patting him on the cheek.

Ralph let out a bellow, "Wot are youze doin'?" and with that took a swing and hit Bruce right between the eyes.

"Thunk!" and the budding Doctor dropped like a stone.

Ralph hauled himself to his feet and looked down at the still form of the young Jackeroo, "I thought he was gunna kiss me, said Ralph. It's not my fault I whaked 'im."

"That's enough cricket for today Ralph," said Jacko as the hulking cook from Engonnia patted him on the shoulder.

"Yeh, that's enough cricket for today. Let's call it a draw it's time for a beer," echoed the crowd of sweating cricket lovers.

The cricket crowd started to drift away now that the fun was over. No dead bodies and Jacko was not in gaol for murder.

In no time the paddock was empty of spectators and cricketers except for two forlorn figures.

Bruce was getting to his feet and shaking his head to clear it of all the buzzing going on.

"Gidday Rusty wherez everybody gone? Is it my turn to bat?" Asked Bruce with a dazed look on his face.

"Nah Bruce they've all scarpered to the pub, the games over and it's a draw."

“A draw, I musta missed something,” said Bruce obviously still recovering from Ralph’s blow to his forehead.

“C’mon mate and let’s go and have a beer,” grinned Rusty.

“I can’t mate I’m only seventeen and they won’t allow me to have a drink until I am twenty one.”

Don’t worry about it Bruce just keep yor head down when you are in the bar. The two friends set off to the Pub and Bruce was moaning ....

“Jeez, I missed out on batting, I coulda done real well even against that monster bowler with the green singlet,” grizzled Bruce.

“Consider yerself lucky you didn’t have to do any, that Jacko is rough mate,” said Rusty.

CHAPTER 6

Country Tennis Match

"Bugger, I wish that dratted bugger Bruce would stop whistlin' that tune, it's drivin' me crazy!" griped one of the Jackeroos one morning as he was bent over the trough having a shave.

"Just what is that infernal tune anyway?"

"Well Bludger I think it is the current favourite on the top 10 on radio called Personality sung by Ray Price and Bruce reckons it's his theme song," smirked Rusty.

"Theme song whaddaya mean?"

"Well Bruce is in love ... and he reckons he has a lot of personality, and he is going to need plenty too, if you ask me."

"Bruce is in I love, who would be crazy enough to love Bruce?" laughed Whippy.

"Miss Lilly of course, the boss' daughter's friend from Sydney. Tho' she doesn't know Bruce, she has never met him. "

"Oh, it's kinda one sided then, I hadda girlfriend like that once," nodded Razza knowingly.

"Well he will need more than a tune to get him to be a couple with that sheila, that's for sure."

"Sheila, whose she," said Bruce whistling away on the second stanza of Personality coming in on the tale end of his mate's conversation.

"Oh, cut it out will ya!"

"Yeh, Bruce give us a rest, and we weren't talkin' about sheila but lovely Lilly up at the big house."

"Lilly, Lillee, Lillie" said Bruce trying out the sound of his sweetheart's name, as he turned to the mirror to admire his reflection and give a last minute comb through his Brylcreemed locks.

“Yeh, give it a rest Bruce, yor making us all sick,” said Bludger looking at Bruce gazing at himself in the mirror with a wide smile on his face.

“She doesn’t stand a chance Bludger when she sees me she can’t hope to resist me, you handsome man,” smirked Bruce giving himself a wink and a toothy smile.

“We’re off to the tennis in town Bruce and you will have a chance of seeing Lilly there as everybody for miles around is coming in to see the fun.”

Bruce’s eyes lit up and his heart started to beat a little faster. Thinking of the chance to meet his long distance love. Never mind that he could not play tennis too well, in fact only having a few lessons, love would prevail.

All the scruffy gang from Booleroo drove up to the red dust tennis court to try their luck. It would be one set per match until the grand final and Bruce was overcome with joy when he was told he would be playing with the lovely Lilly.

“Jeez, Golly wot luck I can just imagine Lilly and I winning the doubles,” said Bruce to no one in particular.

“Who said anything about doubles you are playing against Lilly, you twit,” said Bludger.

“Ah, Jeez, it’s not true it can’t be,” moaned the besotted Bruce.

The announcement came over the Tannoy, “Alright everybody listen up, the list has been drawn up and we have Miss Lilly and Bruce the Jackeroo from Booleroo station to start off as the first singles match of the day.”

“Oh, Jeez I’m for it now lend me yor racquet mate, I can’t beat her it would upset her,” and with that cry from the heart and with slumped shoulders and a sigh Bruce walked out onto the court to meet his doom.

In the distance he saw a vision in loveliness. Lilly was in her tennis gear and didn’t she look ravishing.

Her hair pulled back in a pony tail and with her lips reddened with lipstick showing her blue eyes and lovely face and with a short white skirt, close fitting shirt and tanned legs and short white socks; all this sight of loveliness set Bruce’s heart beating as if it would burst.

Lilly threw the ball in the air and with one sweep hit the ball a wallop and before Bruce knew it the white blur was racing towards him getting bigger and bigger until it passed him with a thrumming sound.

Bruce swung too late, the ball whizzed by with a thrumming sound

He gave a belated swing of his racquet as the ball rocketed past and with a sinking heart he knew that he had no fear of beating Lilly in fact he worried that he would be in for a drubbing.

After a few serves, his hopes were dashed that Lilly would go easy on him and lob a few easy ones as another serve rocketed over the net but this time he managed to hit the ball and over the net it went. Bruce was so surprised that he stopped to have a look and with one bound Lilly hit the ball with a strong return which flashed by Bruce, who was still standing there with his mouth open.

Bruce looked over at Lilly after he was thrashed. Bruce was definitely giving up tennis

In no time Bruce found that the scorer called out "Five nil" and he knew that one more game and his ordeal would be over.

Swish, whiz and a blur of white tennis balls and it was 6 to nil, in Lilly's favour.

It was over. To Bruce the match was over in a flash. Lilly had slaughtered him. His sweetheart had hurt him deeply. With a saddened heart and slumped shoulders Bruce exited the court, knowing that his fervour for Lilly had like a candle's flame in a wind, flickered and gone out.

He sighed, never more could he feel the same way about Lilly, love had died and Bruce walked towards his mates who had the good sense to not say a word about the match and their friend's one sided loss to the beautiful blond.

Lilly was in the meantime at the other end of the tennis court gaily laughing and being congratulated by her friends.

Just one pat on the back and a quiet, "You gave it your best Bruce, never mind," came from Cheryl the Boss' daughter as she walked past.

Bruce gave a rueful smile and reminded himself that he hit a couple but promised to himself that he would never ever take up a tennis racquet ever again.

He sat there in the blazing sun and watched the next match which had started.

Yes it had to be didn't it? It was Ralph from the Stock and Station Agents and he looked as usual the perfect sportsman.

Noticing where Bruce was glowering Rusty said, "I bet Ralphie is a tennis champ."

And Rusty was correct. Ralph took the match in no time 6 nil and returned to his seat after the match without any sign of sweat or effort. He sat there and basked in the radiance of victory and allowed his fellow humans to gaze upon his radiance.

Bruce and the spectators looked upon this picture of health with the white toothed smile and shining hair newly brilliantined with Brylcreem and the tennis shorts showing off fine well muscled calves.

Bruce hated him with a passion.

"He's got a good chance of winning the grand final," said someone near Bruce.

Bruce didn't even turn around to see who has spoken but kept his head down and frowned.

And at the end of the day the grand final was between Ralph, Mr. Perfect and Miss Lilly from Booleroo. Ralph was victorious then and the closely contested match see sawed between Lilly and Ralph until Ralph was victorious.

However, Ralph earned a few more points of dislike from the Enngonia menfolk for beating their sweetheart Lilly. He was not a popular winner as all present were barracking for the lovely blond headed blue eyed nymph from Booleroo.

"Ah, I could watch her for ever, seeing that neat figure runnin' around showing her tanned legs what do you think?" said Whippy

He was met with stony silence and turned to see Bruce with his head still cast down and his face a bright red.

"Ah, so that is how love dies," said Whippy with a wink to Rusty and the two Jackaroos smiled.

CHAPTER 7

Bruce Finds Love

I found myself sinking into the softness of her.

My arms were around her and I was kissing her as if my last breath was about to take place.

Her warmth and soft skin was a delight to me.

We stopped kissing so passionately and drew apart for a short while as if to take breath.

I gazed upon her lovely face and saw how her lips were slightly parted as she drew in a breath and exhaled lightly. She was a delight to me and her beauty glowed in the moonlight.

We held hands as we sat together and watched the waves at Bondi from the light surf roll onto the shore and recede again and do it again and again as it had been doing for millions of years.

I cannot remember what we talked about but it seemed that we meshed as one and I did not feel shy at all, which was a change for me. The only girl I had really spoken to was my sister and she didn't count.

I settled back and lay down on the sand and looked up at the sky where low clouds were scudding across the face of the moon. My delightful companion lay down beside me and I watched her as if in slow motion turn to me and roll over and looked deeply into my eyes.

Closer her lips came to mine and I opened my mouth to kiss her fervently delighting in the softness of her kisses

I felt her moist lips and she then playfully licked my cheek in slow long strokes. I laughed and rather enjoyed the feeling of the smoothness of her tongue against my skin.

For some reason I was glad I had not started shaving yet and my cheek was smooth and the roughness of a beard would not be rasping her delicate tongue.

He looked down at the little dog and was rewarded by a smile and a wagging tail

Suddenly I heard a clamouring bell harshly ringing and I wildly sat up thinking that the surf life saving club nearby had rung a warning bell.

I opened my eyes and the harsh light of day shocked me into wakefulness. The ringing was the cook rousing us all to get ready for an early start by hitting an old tire iron on a bit of scrap iron hung up near the cook house by a bit of rusty chain.

I realized that the Boss' daughter's Fox Terrier, Spot, was sitting on my chest and licking my cheek. The little black and white dog was smiling from ear to ear and I patted him on his crown.

"Ar getorfwillya Spottie?"

The bell kept on ringing and what a racket

“C’mon Brucie wake up mate brekkie will be on soon,” yelled one of my mates as he rushed past on his way to the sink with a towel around his neck for a quick scrub.

Spot was unceremoniously pushed to the floor and I wiped my wet cheek, and gave a shudder as to what germs I had now living in great colonies on the side of my face.

I jumped up and found my towel draped over the foot of my bed and joined the rush to the bathroom shed with all the other Jackeroos.

“Where had my beautiful companion from last night disappeared to?”

“Where oh where had my lover gone?”

Of course it was all a dream, and here I was in the gathering heat of an Australian summer far from my home at Bondi and until a few minutes ago I was lying on my cot in the shearer’s quarters on Booleroo sheep station.

“C’mon Bruce, get a move on and giveus a loan of your soap,” yelled Skeeter.

CHAPTER 8

Jackie Goes Missing

"Jeez it's hot," grizzled Bruce from Bondi to no one in particular.

"Ar stop yer whingin' Brucie," growled Skeeter the diminutive Jackeroo from Trangie.

"Yeh, keep yor hat on mate else the sun will fry your brains," sniggered Bluey the new chum from Lord knows where.

Jackie was the first aboriginal that he had seen up close

Bruce was sitting on the top fence railing overlooking the scenery at Booleroo Sheep Station. The railed fence enclosed a large holding yard filled with about 500 sheep and the jostling bahing and bleating mob below were kicking up clouds of dust.

Flies buzzed around the heads of Bruce and his jackeroo mates while the crows arked away in the surrounding trees. The sun of midday blazed down bathing all below in a spotlight of white light that bleached the scene as if the colours had all faded.

Yes it was hot but it is always hot out the back of Bourke in November and the sheep of Booleroo station were due to be shorn as the last of the mob to be rounded up, for the clip.

This last of the station's sheep had been gathered up over scores of square miles as they were "hiding" in the lignum and scrub. Bruce and his Jackeroo mates had painstakingly rounded them all up on horse back and gathered them in the sheep pens beside the shearers hut for the shearers to do their thing. The sheep would be herded into the shed, shorn and then tipped bleating down the chute about half the size they went in.

"I never thought the sheep would look so skinny wivout their wool," said Bruce half asleep from the heat.

"Ar, pull yor head in Brucie," came a half hearted reply from one of the lads.

"It's alright fer you fellas but I have never been to the country before and it all is so different from Bondi beach," grizzled Bruce.

Bruce was ignored and no doubt the fellows were all thinking about the delights of being at Bondi beside the green sea and the white clad waves with all the beaut sheilas ....

Bruce eventually became sick of looking at the sheep and glanced to his left to look along the railing fence at his mates perched there. He noticed sets of brown arms burned dark by the sun and right at the end of the row a couple of arms that were different. They were a dusty dark brown almost black in tone.

Bruce craned around to see who owned the arms and almost fell off the fence but windmilled his arms and eventually regained his precarious balance.

“Who’s that blackfella along there, I’ve never seen an aboriginal before, well not up close anyway,” whispered Bruce to his mate Whippy.

“You mean Jackie don’t yah,” was the reply.

“Oh that’s his name where did he spring from?”

“Yeh, he’s a full blood and Mr Fisher hired him the other day to show the local elders that he was interested in helping them and provide some jobs for the fellows in the tribe. Anything to keep ‘em outa trouble ya see. Anyhow hop down and we will go over and say gidday.”

The two chums jumped down and sidled over to Jackie who looked down at them. His face was shaded from the sun by a wide brimmed hat and his eyes were almost invisible in the deep eye sockets. There was not even a glint and it was difficult to see if the man was looking at them or had his eyes closed. It was most disconcerting.

“Gidday Jackie I’s like yah to meet Bruce from Bondi,” said Whippy sweeping his hand at Bruce and waving a few score flies away at the same time.

You get pretty good at fly waving out on Booleroo station.

“Yeh gidday Jackie,” said Bruce with a big grin.

Jackie clambered down from where he was sitting and held his hand out to Bruce for a shake.

“Hello Brudder howz yer goin’,” said Jackie and rewarded Bruce with a dazzling smile of huge white teeth in his black face.

The three Jackeroos sat down in the shade and with windmilling arms to ward off the flies fell into a conversation. They discussed what Jackie had been employed for and found that like them he had duties as varied as mustering the sheep, repairing the fences and caring for the sheep.

They eventually got around to the subject they all enjoyed and that was the horses they rode. The boys spent some time on this subject and eventually the little group split up with the promise to catch up again the next day.

The morning was announced by the usual bashing of the piece of scrap iron on an old piece of car that was hanging by a chain near the cookhouse.

The clanging awoke the Jackeroos and they all gathered at the trough to have a wash before breakfast all except Jackie.

“Hey mate I wonder where Jackie has got to, has anyone seen Jackie this morning?” yelled Whippy as he looked around scratching his head.

The chorus of half asleep replies in the negative was answer enough.

“Jeez I wonder if he is alright, I will go and have a look for him and if he’s still asleep I will get him goin’,” said Bruce over his shoulder as he trudged off back to the hut where all the crew had their bunks.

There was short pause and then the door of the hut banged open and Bruce came out running back to the boys by the trough waving a shirt and trousers he had in one hand.

“Look here fellas .... Jackie’s clothes but he he’s gorn,” yelled Bruce in excitement.

Whippy took charge and suggested they have their breakfast and see the foreman and let him know that their newest recruit Jackie had shot through.

“Jeez he never did anything and he has gorn already,” said Bruce.

“Nah couldn’t have he must have had a good reason to leave. He must have a sick mother or something. I reckon we should ride on over to the Aboriginal’s camp and check to see if they know anything. Wot do you reckon?” Queried Whippy who seemed to have more sense than the other Jackeroos.

With that Whippy and Bruce saddled up their respective mounts and ambled off through the scrub to the blackefellas camp down by the tank about two miles from the homestead.

They eventually came to the camp which consisted of a group of humpies and shacks made from corrugated iron, old wheat bags and bits of scrap plywood. A fire smoked in the clearing before the camp and various members of the tribe sat around while the children noisily played football with a ragged ball that had seen better days. Dogs came at them in a rush barking and wagging their tails in welcome, what a noisy greeting. The two Jackeroos rode up and looked down at an old lady and asked her if she had seen Jackie but the old woman shrugged and waved them away.

The camp was a hive of activity

"Jeez she wasn't too helpful was she?" said Bruce.

"Nah don't worry about it mate, she most probably does not understand English too much and we shoulda found someone younger."

They clip clopped over to a few young children and asked them if they had seen Jackie but the little urchins just laughed and ran away.

"Not having much luck are we, let's try them over there," smiled Whippy.

In the shade sitting over under a tree were a group of the tribe's finest with their wide brimmed hats shading their faces.

As the two Jackeroos brought their horses to a halt, Whippy called, "Gidday fellas have ya seen Jackie we were going out today to do a bit of work and he seems to have shot through?"

One of the men raised his head and smiled a wide white smile and his big teeth flashed in his dusky face.

"Gidday whitefella, yeh Jackie has gone."

"Gorn?" echoed Whippy and Bruce.

"Yeh he has gone walkabout and won't be back for a few months," was the reply.

"Walkabout?" said the two Jackeroos in unison.

"Yeh he asked me to let you know if you came by and make sure that you remind the boss man to send his wages down."

"Wages?" said Whippy.

"He only was at Booleroo for a day and he has gorn," said Bruce.

"Yeh wages, send 'em down to us and we will make sure he gets 'em," said the young tribesman with a sleepy smile.

The two Jackeroos rode off into the scrub while the sun beating down on their shoulders and the flies perched there for the ride having a drink from the sweat in their shirts.

All that could be heard was the flies buzzing away and a hoot of laughter behind them from the group of aboriginals under the tree.

"Happy mob of galahs," said Whippy.

"Yeh, not too helpful," sniffed Bruce.

CHAPTER 9

Bruce Is A Great Help

"Here you are fellas, the generator has gone bung again so no power for the lights," yelled Blackie the Foreman as he entered the hut while holding in each hand a kerosene fuelled hurricane lamp.

All this news was met with groans from all present and a few muttered obscenities from the darkened hut.

"......... and Jacko ......the cook also is having trouble in the kitchen and needs one of yerz to help 'im," and this announcement too was met with even louder groans from the captive audience in the dark.

All of the dark forms in the hut feebly illuminated by the flickering light of the hurricane lamps stirred themselves and an anonymous voice from the darkness announced, "Bruce would be happy to help Blackie."

This news was met with loud guffaws and sniggering from the bunch of comedians that made up the inhabitants of the hut.

"Oh Jeez fellas that's not fair," came the quavering voice from Bruce.

"Thanks Bruce for volunteering you will be a great help for the cook, he will really appreciate it, but remember don't get him angry," said Blackie.

"Angry, angry, he's always angry, especially after that cricket match" moaned Bruce, who was rather frightened of the six foot five inch cook who weighed in at a scale breaking twenty stone.

Bruce reported for duty the next morning at the cook house and was immediately shouted at that he was late and the cook was up and about at four a.m. to get the breakfast ready and bake the bread and butcher a sheep and

"Yammer, yammer, yammer, the next thing he will tell me is that he rounded up a whole herd of cattle and made 'em into steaks," moaned Bruce.

Bruce finished his duties as quick as he could and thankfully escaped to his real duties of hunting down some ewes in the top paddock.

Clip clopping over the hard baked ground set Bruce to thinking. There was absolutely no grass on the ground. Any grass that was there in the wet season had long been eaten by the sheep and native animals or dried up and blown away.

"I wonder what the sheep are eatin' I s'pose they are skinny under all that wool," mused Bruce, as he did not have much of an idea about country life having come from the beachside suburb of Bondi only a few months previously in search of adventure.

Bruce had turned eighteen recently and he and his mates from Booleroo sheep station had celebrated in the usual manner by piling into the ute and torn off up the road to celebrate their friend's birthday.

The rough country boys of Booleroo looked for any excuse for a few beers at the Enngonia hotel and Bruce's day was as good as any.

Of course a few beers turned into a flood and many of the Jackeroos when they made their way back to the shearers hut at Booleroo were very much worse for wear the next morning.

In fact the clanging of the cook's tire iron on a bit of scrap iron hung near the cookhouse to announce breakfast sent many of the boys into a spasm of pain as hangovers were the common affliction suffered that morning.

Interestingly the only one who was bright and breezy and up with the crows to have his fried eggs and bacon and tea and toast with marmalade was Bruce and that is because he was eighteen he was not old enough to drink at the Pub he had to be 21.

"Jeez am I glad I didn't drink nuthin 'cept lemon squash, gidday handsome," said Bruce with a big grin and a wink at his image in the fly spotted mirror on the wall as he tucked into a good breakfast.

His only companion was the giant cook in the kitchen, through the fly screen door, where he was shouting furiously at war with his pots and pans vowing that all the wasted food would be made into huntsmen's pie the next day.

"Be damned if I will waste anything on youse @##$$%^&^&," yelled the red faced and sweating ogre from the heat of the kitchen.

Bruce sat there eating his breakfast as fast as he could hoping that the six and a half foot of monster cook would not come and find him. He quickly downed his breakfast and sprinted out the door to get his horse ready for a days work.

Later Bruce and his trusty steed were jogging along and heading out into the top paddock to seek any ewes hiding in the scrub. With the sun on his back, and just a few million flies and a brace of black crows in a nearby tree to keep him company, Bruce was content.

Over on the horizon he saw a movement out of the corner of his eye and a mob of roos see- sawed along to be lost in the patches of lignum. It was quiet in the scrub except for the clip clopping of the horse's hooves and the occasional buzzing of a thirsty fly. He felt as if he was the only living thing on the planet, well that is the way he felt, and he was coming to realise that there were some good things about being out in the Australian bush.

Suddenly he heard a dog bark and making his way around a big thicket of scrub he came across two men standing beside a dozen sheep. The dog had been rounding them up and was now barking at him and making his stock horse step sideways to escape the few bites the dog was half heartedly making at his fetlocks.

"Gidday mate," said Bruce to the taller fellow standing there with his mouth open with his hands buried in the fleece of a struggling ewe.

"Gidday yerself," said his companion who was a short fellow with a heavy build and who seemed to be in charge. Like his skinny mate he too had his hands on a struggling ewe as he was lifting it into a truck.

"Wot are youse guys doin'? Are you helpin' with the mustering too? Jeez nobody tells me anything," grizzled Bruce

The shorter fellow held up his hand to stop the flow of words from Bruce and announced, "I suspect they forgot to tell ya you see we are just helpin' with the musterin' and have been asked to deliver a dozen ewes to town for the butcher."

"Oh good oh, do you want a hand?" said Bruce trying to be helpful.

"That would be very kind of yer," said the short fellow with a big smile and turning to his skinny companion said, "Now aint it nice of the young fella here?"

“Yeh wots yer name mate?” said skinny.

“Bruce, and I’m from Bondi; well I was but I am at Booleroo sheep station now and have been learning the ropes since I got here and ......”

“Me names Clyde and this is Bill,” said the shorter of the two men.

“Er, Gidday fellas,” said Bruce again who was not used to the company of men let alone women.

“How about you give us a hand Bruce as they say more hands makes less work or somethin’ like that,” and the two men hooted with laughter.

Bruce joined in with a few laughs too and the three of them gathered the sheep up in no time and shoved them kicking into the back of the truck.

“Well Bruce you have been a great help, we couldn’t have done the job as well without you,” and with that the two men fell about laughing and slapping each other on the back. In fact Bill almost bent double and smacked his knees with his open hands roaring with laughter.

The men thought it was a great big joke getting a hand with their sheep duffing

“We will be off now, thanks for being such a great help Bruce,” said Clyde, as he hopped up into the cabin of the truck gunned the motor and took off in a cloud of dust.

Bruce stood there with a big smile on his face and waved at the retreating truck; pleased that he could be such a help to his new friends who were also waving gaily from the truck windows.

The bahhing of the sheep in the back and the accelerating truck eventually faded away into the distance.

"Jeez, what friendly happy fellas, it was a pleasure to help them," said Bruce taking his broad brimmed hat off and wiping his dripping forehead with his sleeve.

"Jeez, it's hot .... an' that was a job well done, as Mum would say, 'Doing a job well is a job that's finished or somethin'," said Bruce to the Galahs perched in the shrubs nearby.

The galahs agreed with the usual way in which galahs discuss things with humans and Bruce turned his horse west again to look for more strays.

Later that day Bruce walked his horse and the gathered up ewes he had mustered back to the shearer's quarters and made sure that they were secured safely in the yard, for some cleaning up and a good clip around the hindquarters.

He dismounted and led the stock horse over to a stall in the stables and took the saddle and kit off its broad back. The harness, blanket and gear were hung neatly on pegs and he slung the saddle on a rack for the next day's work. He then rubbed the horse down and gave him a drink and a mouthful of oats and put the feed bag on him.

"There ya are horsie that'l keep youse happy," said Bruce patting the horse.

The horse swished its tail at a few flies in answer as Bruce walked off whistling the tune 'Personality' which he would often say was his theme song, because he reckoned he had plenty of it.

Hitching up his trousers Bruce made his way back to the ablution hut which consisted of an old horse trough a bench with a cake of soap on it and a ragged towel. He quickly washed off all the dust of the day and did not need the towel as it was so hot the water on his face dried by the time he had walked a few yards.

On entering the shearer's quarters Bruce found his mates lying around doing nothing as usual. Skeeter was on his bunk looking at a PIX magazine and smirking at the pinup. Bluey was carving on a piece of wood with his pocket knife making something that to Bruce looked like a piece of wood.

Rusty and Whippy, were having a lemonade that they had saved from one of their trips to town, while they chattered away weighed down by the heat.

“Jeez it’s hot,” said Bruce as he sat down on the step near his mates.

They both looked up and chorused, “Gidday Bruce,” and continued talking.

“Yair them sheep duffers are driving Mr. Fisher to drink I reckon,” said Rusty.

“The bastards have got away with a paddock full of sheep by now I reckon and the local copper is just scratching his ‘ead and telling everyone it is a gang of real smart rustlers. He hasn’t come close to arresting anybody yet,” added Whippy.

“Yeh, stock theft in the region is particularly hard to fix as thieves operate over great areas and over long periods of time. And it is only when farmers bring sheep in for drenching or shearing that the loss is noticed.”

“They have seen signs of a truck and the local black tracker reckons it’s two men one heavy and the other light, judging by their footprints in the dust,” murmured Whippy.

Turning to Bruce Whippy asked, “have you heard or seen anything that would make you suspicious as you have been out and about a lot these last few weeks in the east and south paddocks?”

Opening a bottle of lemonade and guzzled half of it down Bruce settled himself comfortably on the step and exclaimed, “Jeez it’s hot!”

He thought a few moments about Whippy’s question and then shook his head, “Nah I’ve seen nuffink or nobody suspicious mate I reckon nuthin exciting happens here on Booleroo. It’s so boring, I wish I could catch ‘em though there might be a reward I could do with a few quid. Then I could leave here. You know good old Bondi Beach is looking real good from where I’m sittin’ and those sheilas and the waves I dunno which is better....... and....... “

“Bruce, give it a rest!” the two Jackeroos said together as the three sat there sipping their lemonade and thinking about the chance of catching sheep stealers and getting a reward.

"Anyhow nuthin excitin' happens on Booleroo," said Bruce who was determined to have the last word.

CHAPTER 10

The Ghostly Visitors

"How about you stay up tonight Bruce and keep an eye on Mrs. Fisher's garden. Something is eating her flowers and we have to try and catch it. We have tried everything such as rabbit traps but no rabbits. We have put up a wire fence and that has been broken down, so whatever it is its big enough to level a rabbit proof fence."

Mrs. Fisher worked long and hard in her garden and considering the dry climate and the harsh sun she had done quite well, especially with the sun flowers and the chrysanthemums.

The blazing sun beat down on the homestead which made it hard to grow a good garden

"Do yer reckon it's wild pigs?" asked Skeeter, one of the men.

"Nah if it was the ground would be broken up as they use their snouts to dig up the roots and tubers under the ground and there is no sign of that, they make a real mess."

"Er could it be birds then?"

"Come off it mate when the damage is done it is night time and not many birds are out of a night that would eat flowers," replied Blackie.

“Jeez Blackie how can I be of help if I stay up all night?” whinged Bruce.

“Not scared of the dark are you Bruce?” one of the fellows said.

“Er not really it’s just ..... that when I was in Bondi Beach I ....”

“Come on now Bruce Mr. Fisher and his good lady are depending on you to stop the damage in the garden. You can have the next day off but we want youse to stay up tonight and keep your eyes peeled. How about Bluey goes with you to keep you company?”

“Bluey’s no company, getting a conversation outa him is liking squeezing stones,” grumbled Bruce under his breath.

Later that night Bruce and Bluey found themselves sitting with their backs against the homestead’s weatherboard wall with a couple of folded chaff bags under them for comfort, Bruce at one end and Bluey at the other. The bags would keep the cold of the ground from sending their nether regions numb otherwise they would be very uncomfortable.

Bruce had the good sense to bring a bottle of water and a few biscuits to ease thirst and hunger but apart from that he had made little arrangements. Bluey lost somewhere in the dark would have to fend for himself.

“I should have brung a torch to see coz it’s as dark as the inside of a cow,” murmured our hero.

Bruce had all night to sit there and soon he found that he was thinking about things that if he was truthful to himself he would take seriously. He knew he was not brave and also realized for some unfathomable reason that he was indeed afraid of the dark

He knew that there was nothing really out there except a few mobs of rabid feral pigs, packs of wild dogs, fierce aboriginal tribesmen and most probably worse terrors so there was absolutely no chance that he would fall asleep that night.

He waited and waited in the cooling night. “Funny how the bush gets cold after a hot day,” mused Bruce.

He found that when he was alone like this and with nothing to do he let his mind drift and many questions sprang into his mind that had no answers that would spring into his mind.

Bruce thought that this new wave of thinking was a sign that he was possibly growing up or that he had gulped his dinner and had heartburn or something.

"I wonder why I don't have a nick name, everybody has a nick name, I wish I had a nick name, just calling me Brucie is rotten," Bruce found himself thinking.

"I reckon everybody on Booleroo, except the Boss, Mr. Fisher, has a nick name except me. There is Whippy, Rusty, and there is Skeeter and even dopey Bluey has got a nick name. Now mine could be Lover or .... There has got to be a reason. I wonder of it is because my personality is flawed. Don't they like me or is it because they laugh at me?

All these thoughts were going through Bruce's mind and deep down he found he did not like the introspection. He was far happier thinking about girls, Bondi Beach and its delights rather than dwell on what made him tick.

It must have been the early hours of the morning when Bruce was starting to nod off that there was a movement of dark shadows out in the paddock. It was hard to see but the dark shapes drifted in closer and seemingly melted into the fence and spread out amongst the flower beds. Bruce was by this time in a state of almost self hypnosis and did not hear or see anything that would alarm him. Eventually sleep overcame him and he drifted off.

Suddenly Bruce woke with a shock and he heard someone yelling.

"Look at my flowers, they've gone, they are ruined, oh how could this happen and after all my work and why didn't you stop them?"

Bruce sat up with a start and his heart almost missed a beat, as being shocked awake like he was, made him go all weak at the knees. He stood up and peered over the chewed and tattered heads of the flowers that the night before had been magnificently rearing their beautiful heads to the sky.

Mrs. Fisher and her daughter Cheryl were standing on the other side of the garden bed glowering at him as his disheveled head appeared above the ruined flower stems.

"Yes you, why didn't you stop them?" yelled Mrs. Fisher who was red in the face.

Bruce's disheveled head rose up above the ruined flower stems

"What have you done to Mum's flowers?" yelled Cheryl whose light green eyes looked like gooseberries in her red face.

Everybody has a red face this mornin' thought Bruce and luckily for him had the sense not to speak out loud.

"Yes, what has been going on here Bruce and you to Bluey, whose big head had also risen like a whale from the depth of the ocean, you were suppose to have scared off what ever was eating them and now look at them they are ruined and it's all your fault," said Mrs. Fisher with a red face and scowling brow.

"Er, gidday Mrs. Fishuh, and er Cheryl howaryerz?" smiled Bruce looking down at his feet and kicking a few divots of soil out of the flower bed.

"Yair gidday Missus," mumbled Bluey.

"Don't you try and get out of this you two it's all your fault," huffed Mrs. Fisher frowning severely at the hapless Jackeroos.

"I dunno, I didn't see nuthin. It must have been ghosts," was Bruce's brilliant reply.

"Yair," said the unhappy Bluey.

"Ghosts, don't be silly there are no ghosts on Booleroo!" yelled Cheryl.

"Well there are now," said Bruce with all the smugness that he could muster, "I told you it wasn't our fault."

"We shall see about that," said Mrs. Fisher ominously as she swung around, "come on Cheryl let's go back to the house we will have a talk to the Foreman about this. It will just not do, I cannot imagine why he would have chosen Bruce and this, gesturing at Bluey ...... to be guards of my beautiful garden."

Bruce and Bluey thought that by now it was best not to say anything and just stood there with smarmy smiles on their faces while watching the Boss's wife march off and see Cheryl swing her large shoulders and follow; both ladies with their noses in the air and their jodhpur clad bottoms swinging along.

Bruce thought that discretion was the better form of valour and decided to retreat to the shearer's quarters. Bluey drifted off and most probably got lost in the wilderness, for all Bruce cared. Just over by the cookhouse he saw his mate Rusty standing there with a towel and soap.

"Gidday Bruce how're you going did you have any luck, did you see anything?"

"Nah, I did not see nuthin and anyhow it is a waste of time now coz all the flowers are gone."

"Gone," said Whippy, "gone where .... has Mrs. clipped em?"

"Nah ghosts I reckon," and Bruce proceeded to tell his mates about the embarrassing conversation he and Bluey had with the two ladies a short time ago.

"It can't be ghosts Brucie," Skeeter announced, "I reckon what we should do is go down to the Blackfellas camp and ask the chief. He may have one of his blokes come back who can do trackin' and be able to see what it was that ate all them flowerz."

"Good idea Skeeter me lad," said the foreman as he entered the hut where most of the drovers were lying around before breakfast.

"I will organize that this arvo and we can then get to the bottom of the mystery."

That afternoon all the Jackeroos, kitchen staff, and Fisher family were gathered in a group near Mrs. Fisher's tattered garden watching a stooped and dark figure walking up and down the garden beds.

"Just lookit that, isn't it marvelous these blackfellas can read signs and it is just like an open book to em they can let you know who has walked by and how long ago how heavy they are and so forth it is amazing?"

Eventually the tribesman wandered over to the group and they all started talking at once and asking him what he had seen.

"Tell us Jackie it must be as plain as the nose on yer face?" said Rusty.

The Blackman looked at Rusty and then turned to Mrs. Fisher, he looked at the crowd, let some dirt run through his fingers, looked at the sky. Scratched his head and said, "It was the spirit of the Bunyip."

There was dead silence from all of the crowd.

Except one of the Jackeroos laughed and said audibly, "I think the black fella is pulling our leg!"

Mr. Fisher thanked Jackie and gave him a pack of cigarettes and a pound of sugar and some tea leaves and the proud native of Australia drifted off down to the camp by the tank.

The foreman said, "You know what I think I would say that the flower eaters are a mob of kangaroos and all they need is a good scare to keep them out, now everybody you heard what Jackie said who is going to stay up tonight and see what it really is that's eating Mrs. Fisher's garden? This time though take a torch!"

Everybody looked at Bruce and then Bluey and all swung away and looked elsewhere as they did not really think that the young Jackeroos were up to the task.

"Phew, I'm glad I don't have to stay up again tonight, I don't like ghosts, one little bit," said a secretly relieved Bruce to no one in particular.

CHAPTER 11

Sally The Sow

Faintly a cry for help could be heard.

There was suddenly dead quiet in the shearer's quarters at Boolaroo sheep station.

"Crickie wots that," said one of the Jackeroos.

"It sounds like trouble to me mate," yelled Whippy.

"C'mon chaps let's go and see we may be able to help," said the Pommie drover who made everybody sick because he always wanted to be a hero.

There was much yelling and pushing as the sweating men got caught up in the door way of the shearers shed but at last they all scrambled out into the sunshine where they were met by the full heat and glare of the sun.

December was not the right weather for Christmas that's for sure especially if you were on Booleroo sheep station out at Enngonia, at the back of Bourke.

The cries for help became louder as the men raced around the homestead and they skidded to a halt when they saw what was happening.

Madame Troubridge, a hairdresser from Dubbo, had come and visited the Boss' wife, Mrs. Fisher and had hurried on down to the outhouse to make a visit. A call of nature, so as to speak.

She must have had food with her because the family pet, Sally the Sow, who was always looking for a feed, had bailed her up in the outside toilet and she could not get out because 400 lbs of giant ravenous pig was waiting for her.

With a lot of huffing and puffing Cheryl and the rest of the Fisher family came running up and all of the crowd of people heard the cry again.

Sally the sow lurked just outside the dunny while Mrs Troubridge cowered inside

“Help,” went the quavering voice from within the outhouse, “please get me out of here”.

“Come on lads grab the pig and we will soon have the problem fixed, eh what?” drawled our lad from England.

Without further prompting the brave Booleroo team jumped on Sally and with loud squealing from the indignant pig, were immediately thrown off.

“I reckon it’s pretty hard to hold down a 400 pound sow,” commented Bruce from Bondi who at this stage was standing there watching the spectacle.

The shearers and then the drovers all piled aboard the pig’s broad back again and Sally shrugged them off effortlessly with an angry squeal for no way were any of these puny humans going to get between her and a meal.

“Hells bells and buggy bells can’t any of youse hold er down!” roared the foreman.

“Oh, Madame Troubridge, do you have any food in there?” called Cheryl, “Sally usually goes after food as that is the only thing that matters to her.”

All of the men standing around laughed at this bit of news and there was a general exchange of information and advice as what was needed to be done to rescue Madame Troubridge.

"Yes I had the last of my chicken sandwich but I swallowed it," came the quavering reply.

"Uh oh .... well open the door Madame Troubridge and show Sally you have nothing in your hands and I am sure she will lose interest."

The door slowly opened and a very dishevelled and red faced dowager lady came into view. She held up two be-ringed hands and showed the hungry pig that she was sandwich-less.

Sadly a very optimistic and hungry pig like Sally was not so easily convinced there was no food available and she jumped as high as she could, a measly 3 inches, to see if there was anything to eat hidden behind Madame Troubridge' broad back.

"Look out!" yelled one of the wags, "she's gunna charge!"

It was at this stage of the unfolding drama that Bruce decided to get involved, he had been watching all the commotion and the lovely old pig was being very badly treated, in his opinion.

"Now listen boys leave Sally alone you are just getting her angry, I can get her calmed down and I will take her back to her pen, she will follow me alright."

Loud laughter and ribald remarks greeted this utterance of Bruce who hitherto had stood idly by watching the ruckus.

"Yeh, she fancies you Bruce, you would appeal to Sally that's for sure, no other girl would have yah" came a laughing comment from one of the members of the herd of humans outside the dunny.

"Oh Bruce we will never get her back to her pen and Dad is just looking for an excuse to send her off to old Shanahan in town to be butchered into hams and things, oh I can't bear it," and Cheryl turned away and started to sob.

Now nothing effects brave young men like a woman's tears and Bruce had a tear in his eye too which he quickly wiped away.

"Jeez dunt worry Cheryl I can fix er."

"Thank you Bruce," said Cheryl with a beaming smile as she turned and looked up at Bruce.

Bruce let out a clucking noise and with a flourish waved an apple that he had in his pocket over the head of Sally.

"I think you have got her attention, and my goodness where on earth did that come from?"

Bruce looks sheepish and said, "I have one every day coz it's the only way I can get a saddle on me horse. He loves apples."

"Oh, well it may be a way to get Sally moving," laughed Cheryl.

And sure enough the giant pig immediately followed Bruce wagging her stubby little tail and sashayed through the gate to her pen. When she had been safely locked away Bruce lobbed the apple into the air and Sally caught it and in a blink it had disappeared.

"Oink."

"Goodonyer Sally old girl that'll fix yer."

Relative peace and quiet now reigned outside the outhouse as the crowd of Jackeroos and Drovers sauntered off. The Fisher family also left holding each plump arm of the hairdresser Madame Troubridge, leaving Bruce and Cheryl alone with Sally the Sow.

"Do yuh reckon that is a smile on er face?" asked Bruce with a smirk pointing at the sow with his chin.

Cheryl turned to look at Sally and then Bruce who she had not really seen until today. He had shown such kindness in first getting all the larrikin stockmen to leave Sally alone and then to lead her gently back to her pen.

What she saw before her was a man of middle height say 5' 10", lean like many men on the land, sandy haired with a smattering of attractive freckles across his cheeks and piercing blue eyes above a straight nose. All in all she wondered just why she had not noticed such an attractive man before.

All she could think was that somehow he had just grown up and matured. No longer did she see a pale gangling youth with an awkward manner; this man was a seasoned Jackeroo, gentle with animals and kind. "I wonder why Lilly did not see what I am seeing," was the thought that briefly went through her mind, "because Bruce certainly had a crush on her."

"Oh Bruce thank you so much I have noticed you are so good with animals; Flossy the mare loves you and Bob the Brumby has even offered to go left or right if you ask nicely, just joking."

"Steady on Cheryl," said Bruce with a mock frown.

" ..... and Spot loves you to,"

"Ahh me old mate Spottie, my cheek was alive with germs after that licking he gave me," laughed Bruce.

"Now I wonder if you could help me, you see Dad wants to send Sally off to the butchers but she has been a pet since we got her as a piglet after the boys went out shooting wild pigs and came back with her. Well she certainly has grown a bit it's only when she wants to follow me into the house does she cause any problems and when I say no she flounces off with a squeal and goes and hides behind the water trough. She is really a lovely girl and just loves to have her belly rubbed."

"Yair who doesn't," said Bruce absentmindedly.

"Oh Bruce you can be quite a joker when you put your mind to it," said Cheryl with a smile as she strolled on back to the house.

Bruce frowned and looked mystified and took off his broad brimmed hat and scratched his head as he walked back to the shearer's quarters.

"Me a joker she's gotta be kidding! But I gotta help her out, it would be rotten if Sally had tah go. Perhaps I should have a talk with Whippy, he usually knows what to do."

CHAPTER 12

After Work At Booleroo

Driving over the paddocks of his friend's property in the Austin A Seven one hot and windless day out on the black soil plains Bruce and his mate Whippy were relaxed and chatting in a desultory way about rural life in general.

Suddenly Whippy stopped the car and drawled, "Look over there Bruce, there is a mob of pigs wanderin' along through the lignum. They look like they are a bit far out so I don't know if it is worth a shot. Say Bruce have you ever used a rifle before?"

"Can't say I have Whippy but I sure would like to have ago at it."

Bruce was surprised he had hit the target and stood there. He remembered to keep his mouth closed though, as there were a few thousand flies about

"Yeh, I've got a rifle in the boot and we can stop just about here and you can have a shoot."

The two chums alighted from the hot and dusty car to a stifling and dusty world. They wandered around to the rear of the grey car and Whippy opened up the boot with a creak of dry and rusty hinges and rummaged around until he found what he was looking for.

The rifle that was pulled out of the pile of dusty rubbish in the boot was indeed a sorry sight. It was an old World War I .303 Lee Enfield and had seen far better days.

"Here you are mate, she'll be alright and all I havetuh do is give her a bit of a rub down and she will be as good as new," said Whippy.

A bit of old burlap sacking was produced and the rifle was freed of some of the detritus. It was no gleaming museum piece but at least you could see the bleached bluing of the barrel and the caked dust and dirt had been rubbed away from the bolt.

Whippy handed over a handful of brass .303 rounds and Bruce retrieved them from the grimy paw of his mate.

He was then shown how to shove a few rounds into the box magazine and Bruce was told to put the chaff bag down on the Austin's bonnet to rest the rifle while he had a shot.

"I reckon you are wasting your time now Bruce as they are a bit far off but just aim into the black line of pigs you see and hope for the best."

"I can see them Whippy and I reckon that should be enough."

All this time the mob of feral pigs were slowly making their way into the distance.

"Bang", Bruce squeezed the trigger as he was told and the rifle kicked.

"Jeez look at them run," said Bruce, as the mob of pigs running fast disappeared into the scrub.

"Well blow me down, you got one mate, that was pretty good shooting are you sure you've never fired a rifle before?" said an excited Whippy.

"That was good alright mate but there were so many of 'em I don't think knocking one over will do much to do any damage to them. There must have been fifty or more of the things."

"Yes, I suppose your right but I just hate them for what they do to the lambs and the damage they cause. Let's get back to the homestead and have a cup of tea before cook clangs the old tire iron for tucker time."

One of the few pleasures Bruce found out on Booleroo station was sitting out under the stars after dinner and yarning with his fellow drovers.

After the cook's latest horrific concoction a drowsy Bruce reclined by the fire trying to digest the dinner whose contents were a bit of a mystery.

His mates were sipping scalding hot cups of tea sweetened by condensed milk and munching on Gingernut biscuits, which were everyone's favourites.

"Snap," went the sound like a .22 rifle shot as someone bit into a rock hard biscuit. Bruce smirked to himself because he was not sure if it was one of his mate's teeth or the rock hard ginger tasting delicacy.

The boys liked nothing more after work than to sit by the fire and have a yarn

“Glad it wasn’t my tooth, coz getting to a dentist out here is not easy and usually the vet does the fixing”, thought Bruce with a shudder.

“The only way to eat these things Bruce is to soak ‘em”, said Skeeter as he sucked on a softened biscuit.

“Good idea Skeeter but you’ve got to be careful though when you do coz if you leave ‘em in too long to soak, then they fall apart and sink to the bottom of yer mug”.

The fire was hypnotic as everyone gazed into the flames and thought wondrous things. All of them found they were baked on their fronts but their backs were freezing.

Out in the Australian bush many of the night’s temperatures hit freezing point or close to it and often you would find of a morning the horse trough with a skin of ice.

This night Whippy had started the yarning off with a casual mention of his childhood and how he ended up as a roustabout on a sheep station.

His one dream was to own a motorbike and muster the sheep with the machine with two wheels rather than being perched high above the ground on a cantankerous stock horse. Especially some of the nags had a mystery parentage and were wild brumbies with a bit of thoroughbred in the mix somewhere.

Razza sniggered at Whippy’s words and whispered to Blackie, “There’s no way that Mr. Fisher would invest in a motorbike to muster sheep. Horses will always be used for this sorta thing, never bikes, that’s for sure.”

All were silent as they digested Razza’s glimmer of sight into the future.

To break the oppressive silence, broken only by the crackle of the flaming logs on the fire, Bluey the dopey drover spoke up.

“You know fellas I wuz an orphan and had no muvver and no farver”, and a few tears slipped down his cheeks as he lapsed back into silence while his shoulders shook a little with suppressed emotion.

Again there was silence from all as they digested this bit of news. For just a minute Bruce felt sorry for Bluey and then shook his head and muttered, “I must be crazy, feeling sorry for that nitwit.”

Bruce spoke out of the side of his mouth to Whippy, "With our mate Bluey I bet that when he was born his parents took one look at him and fled."

Whippy chuckled and agreed saying that it would account for some of Bluey's problems.

Whippy was about to speak up and tell a tale, for as usual when he spoke all the fellows recognised that he made a lot of common sense and usually listened with no interruption. However, this night it was different because while Whippy finished rolling his own smoke and wet it with his lips and searched for a match and before he could open his mouth Bluey decided to have another go.

"Hey fellas do you want to hear a joke"?

"No Bluey," chorused the drovers lying around in the dark.

Bluey laughed and ignored the apparent disinterest in his joke telling prowess, "What is a long thin pole of iron called?"

In the gloom a few snarls greeted this pronouncement and Bruce was good natured enough to ask, "No Bluey, what is a long thin pole of iron?'

"Why it's a piece of wire, that's what," guffawed dopey the now ex friend of everyone present.

A groan was heard from all and for a minute or two after that piece of silliness there was another lengthy silence until Skeeter spoke up and asked with a yawn, "Where did you get that one from Bluey"?

"I made it up yer see, I was riding along thinking of nothing much when it sprang into me brain. I have been working on jokes you see coz there is not much to do when you are out there looking for silly sheep lost in the scrub."

Again there was silence for a while until they absorbed Bluey's announcement of almost rational thought and someone murmured that they did not know what was sillier the sheep or Bluey.

To get everyone talking again after the shock of Bluey's joke to the nervous system, one of the boys brought out a bottle of OP Rum and asked if everyone would like a wee drop. Snigger snigger .... and a few poured a measure into their sweetened tea and one stirred some into his enamel mug added hot water and some condensed milk.

“No matter which way you have this stuff,” said Whippy with a grimace, “it tastes terrible but it sure keeps you warm”.

Lying back looking up at the millions of stars scattered like silver sand on a black blanket and with the frosty blackness of the night around him Bruce put his back to the fire and warmed himself.

He spoke quietly to Razza beside him, “it’s like toast ya know you’ve gotta do yourself on both sides to keep warm’.

“Yeh, the old timers tell you that the best way to have a camp fire is instead of one big fire you have two small ones and sit between them that would be the best bet.”

The local tribe’s representative at this gathering of eagles smiled and his white tombstone teeth gleamed in the light from the fire. “How about I play youse another song boys”, announced Jackie and with that he sat back and strummed a chord or two on his guitar.

Someone chuckled in the gloom and was heard to say, “That song sounded the same as the first one but the words wuz different. Come on Jackie give us a tune and none of that corroboree stuff you insist on singing. It is all one note and sounds like a million blowflies”.

Jackie roused himself and sucked on his cigarette and placed it firmly in the corner of his mouth out of harms way and launched into the favourite song of many lads in the country, “The Wild Colonial Boy”.

There was a wild Colonial Boy,
Jack Doolan was his name,
Of poor but honest parents,
He was born in Castlemaine.
He was his father’s only hope
His mother’s pride and joy,
and dearly did his parents love

Jackie droned the song as the boys all joined in with various degrees of success.

When the song was over there was loud laughter and a few rude comments. Blackie the foreman smiled and said, "Thanks Jackie that was good stuff but you still managed to make it sound like an Aboriginal Corroborre, all one note and a lot of singing through your nose."

Loud guffaws greeted this announcement and Jackie laughed too and put down his guitar to light his cigarette which had gone out while he was singing.

Skeeter rolled over and cleared his throat. "Fellas, I have been workin' here for awhile now and I just want you to know I reckon you are the best bunch of ratbags a man could ever meet."

"Thanks mate," came the voice from the dark, "faint praise indeed."

Skeeter laughed and waived away a giant moth that was dive bombing him before it continued its circuitous journey to the fire. "Seriously though fellas I can only take so much of this way out here lookin' after the silliest animal ever made by God, a bloody sheep, and then I am off to the big smoke to see a crowd of people and go to the pictures and see a good looking sort and take her out and …."

"Yes, said Bruce, I agree coz I miss Bondi and I can't wait to get back there and have a surf and meet some sheilas and …."

A burst of laughter greeted Bruce's monologue which ground to a halt because all had heard it many times and most virtually knew it all off by heart.

"Well I reckon we have a bonza girl here on Booleroo," cut in Whippy. "I reckon that Cheryl, is a great girl and she has a nice way about her."

Loud giggles greeted this announcement and a few gave each other a dig in the ribs and winked in the gloom.

"Aw, Whippy has a sweetheart," smirked Bluey. "Good luck to ya coz she is a real toughie especially when Bruce 'n I didn't know what was eatin' her Mum's flowers and she yelled at us. Golly was she rough!"

"There you are she is smart too because she recognised a blockhead when she sees one," laughed Whippy and all joined in to the discomfort of Bluey who did not quite work out whether Whippy was complimenting him or criticising him.

The chill of the night was seeping into everybody's bones and one by one they drifted away from the fire to seek warmth in their cots.

Silence reigned and Bruce and his chum Whippy were left by the fire which by now had died down to just a few embers of red.

"It's gunna be a hot one tomorrow Bruce, I reckon."

"Jeez it's always hot here Whippy, I reckon we orta turn in then," said Bruce as he clambered to his feet.

Whippy scraped the soil and ashes over the remaining embers and there was darkness as a cold wind blew in from the paddocks bringing with it a whiff of the sheep deposits in the yard.

"Night mate".

"Yeh Bruce".

CHAPTER 13

Goodbye To Booleroo

"I heard that Sally the Sow doesn't have to pay a visit into town to the butcher's," said Skeeter to Bruce the Jackeroo from Bondi.

"Yairz, from what I heard Cheryl threatened to leave home and marry a Pommie if her Dad sent the pig off for a change into ham, bacon and pork sausages. .... and anyhow her Dad has now changed his mind so the pig does not have to leave us and we have a happy Cheryl."

"Pfhizzz and thonk" ..... went the whip.

"I will never get the hang of this Skeeter the way in which the other blokes can crack that whip. When I do it the thing either clips me on the ear or takes my hat off," moaned the trainee Jackeroo.

When Bruce practiced with the stock whip everybody ran for cover

Skeeter nodded at his friend and took a lazy swing at the can on the fence and with a graceful sweep of his arm his whip snaked out and flicked the can off the post with a loud.

"KER KRACK!"

"That's how you do it me lad," laughed Skeeter, "anyhow I don't think we will have much use for a stock whip on a sheep station but it is good fun .... Ah common Bruce it is practice mate. You have been up here what, over two years now; an' you should be able to do it by now."

"All I know is that when I get the whip out and start swingin' it around everybody takes cover," said Bruce

"Swishhh .... Pfhizzz and thonk..... "

Skeeter laughed at Bruce's fisser of an effort to crack the whip as he ruefully rubbed his unshaven chin, "yep I can sympathise with the lads,

mate, coz I can well remember the time you had a go with the stock whip and wrapped yourself up in it and all most fell over. When we stopped running and came out when the coast was clear, we all had a big laugh."

Later that night Bruce phoned home to his family in far away Bondi on the party line. After a wait when he had to listen to Mrs. Gobbers down the road talking about her chickens, Bruce eventually got through to his home when his mother answered the phone.

"Hello, is that you Bruce?" came the faint voice from the speaker.

"Yairz Mum owaryou, I am due for a holiday soon and I thought I would come on home and have a swim and a bit of a holiday."

"That'll be lovely Bruce dear I will tell your Dad and he will be so pleased to see you. I can cook your favourite dinner a roast lamb with all the trimmings just as you like it."

"Jeez, Mum if you don't mind can you make it roast beef, coz we have had lamb till the cows come home out here on Booleroo."

"Alright Bruce that will be fine," came the faint voice down the line.

"I will get a train from Dubbo and be down next Sunday so I will see yuz then Mum."

"All right Bruce that will be lovely we will see you then."

"Hey Whippy the next time you are driving down to Dubbo can you give me a lift, I am going on leave?" yelled Bruce to his mate who was across the room mending some harness.

"I am leaving in a few days so you are in luck, you can hitch a ride with me Bruce," said Whippy.

Well that was it. Bruce had organised transport and a holiday in very quick time. It was only a few days later that he found himself lounging in the cabin of the utility truck as it made its way south to the railhead at Dubbo, for his train trip to Sydney and home.

The two chums motored on down the Mitchell Highway; their first stop was at the Trangie Pub for a beer and a counter lunch then off they went in quick time towards Dubbo.

"You had better watch out for them sheilas when you get to Bondi Beach Bruce," yelled Whippy over the noise of the engine and the rushing wind as they sped along.

Bruce laughed at this and ruefully thought that at the great age of nineteen, going on twenty he should have a girlfriend by now. However, living at Booleroo miles from anywhere sure made it hard to meet anyone and he smiled when he thought about the one who loved him the most which was good old Spottie the Fox Terrier house dog.

Upon arrival at Dubbo Bruce was eventually dropped off at the railways station and after an exhausting trip he arrived back home, dusty and dishevelled. His Mum greeted him at the door and he had to endure the hugs and kisses that only a loving Mum can give. He was then ushered down the hall to the kitchen where he was plied with a plateful of pikelets and lamingtons and a cool GI drink.

"There you are love, all your favourites," smiled Mum.

"Jeez thanks Mum I have been really looking forward to all this and to get on down to the beach to have a surf, it was pretty dry out at Booleroo."

CHAPTER 14

Bruce's New Career

The next morning Bruce yelled out a quick farewell to his Mum and hotfooted it down to Bondi Beach a block or two away. He couldn't wait to visit the beach and run, walk and feel the sand between his toes; surf, swim look at the girls and have an ice cream.

In no time Bruce arrived at his destination paused and just stared at the beautiful view. There it was his first glimpse of the sea after two years. Stretched before him was the sparkling blue of the Tasman Sea in the sunshine with the steady roar of the waves as they rolled in from across the far horizon.

He hurried on down and quickly walked out on to the beach, it was good to feel the sand between his toes. The water was clear and felt icy on his bare legs. The white caps and the rolling surf was what he had been waiting for and dreaming about for over two years and now he was here back on his beloved Bondi Beach.

No longer was Bruce that young boy who lived the life of a Smart Aleck. He had matured in those two years working in the country, after all who would not. He thought of his days yarning with his mates, driving into Enngonia for a cool drink at the pub. All this was streaming through his head like a fast tracking movie film.

Bruce hurried over to the attendant who was hiring out surf boards and Bruce paid his two shillings and walked on down to the water's edge ready to do a bit of riding the board on the waves.

He stood there breathing in the smell of salt, hearing the cries of children at play and the steady roar of the waves as they rolled in. Gone were the sounds of flies buzzing, the clip clopping of his stock horse's hooves and the forlorn cry of the crows.

This is what he loved.

The first shock of the cold water revived his senses and he paddled swiftly out beyond the surf and lay there on his board and looked into the clear water where just twenty feet or so below was the sand. The water was like glass and he could easily see little fish flash past with a glint of silver.

Bruce soon relaxed and just rested there with his eyes closed and felt the sensation of the water rising and falling while the sun warmed his back and legs.

The motion of the board on the waves eventually made him a little woozy and he stopped floating there and sat up on the board to search for a suitable wave to ride. In no time he saw one which looked perfect and he started paddling quickly towards shore. He then felt himself lifted and at speed and raced down the face of the wave.

"Ahhh, my first wave, Jeez it's like riding a bike, once you learn you never forget, was the thought flitting into his mind as he sped shoreward."

He had dreamed about this moment for two years, surfing at his beloved Bondi

Bruce had a wonderful time that morning.

After wearing himself out surfing he returned his board to the attendant and gathered up all his gear and set off to find a vendor to buy an ice cream. Laughing to himself Bruce wondered if the cool sweetness of the Peters Ice-Cream was worth dreaming about all those dusty hot months and it sure was. Vanilla flavour too was his favourite.

Licking away industriously Bruce strolled along near the rocks on the south end when he thought now was as good a time as any. He walked back to the centre of the beach and made his way to the Surf Life Saving Club building to make enquiries about joining the Club as a life saver.

Upon entering the office he was greeted by a pretty girl sitting behind a table reading a Woman's Weekly magazine. She put the magazine down when he greeted her and rewarded him with a beaming smile.

"Jeez she's a corker," thought Bruce and returned the pretty girl's smile with one of his own.

Bruce looked sideways at the girl, she was clad only in a two piece swimming costume and was lightly tanned and she was bumpy in all the right places as far as he could see.

"Boy is she a good sort," thought Bruce to himself.

"Hello, I'm Jane, what can I do for you?"

"Er, Bruce from Booleroo, I was thinking of joining up as a life saver with Bondi Beach Club," mumbled Bruce.

"Alright just fill out this application and we can sign you up," said the beautiful girl pushing across a form with a pencil.

While Bruce completed the paperwork he and Jane chatted away and she was really interested when she saw that he had put Jackeroo in the occupation box.

Bruce obviously besotted by the lovely Jane asked her why she was at the Surf Life Saving Club and she told him that she was just helping on the weekend as during the week she worked for her father at the local hotel at Bondi.

Upon learning that Jane was the heiress of a Pub Bruce brightened up even more and asked her if there were any jobs available.

“Now Jane I reckon I could do a good job at the Pub, what do you think?

To his relief Jane thought that he would be excellent and gave him another one of her sparkling white beaming smiles.

“I wonder if she likes me,” was the thought that ran through Bruce’s mind. “Nah, can’t be, I am never that lucky.”

However, Bruce was wrong this time because Jane really did think he was very nice and interesting.

“I hope he likes animals,” was the thought that flashed through her mind and she said, “How about you come on down with me to the hotel after I finish here and you can meet Dad and talk to him about the hotel and see if there is a job available?”

Bruce hung around yarning with Jane until 5 o’clock closing time and they then both strolled down to the Pub a few blocks away. Bruce took this opportunity to have a real good look up close at Jane and he was absolutely smitten.

Upon entering the hotel’s office to meet Jane’s father a large dog came bounding out to greet them with loud barks and jumped up and down as if she had not seen Jane for many months.

Jane knelt down to pat the Alsatian who ignored her and sidled over to stand beside Bruce and look up at him adoringly.

“Gidday old girl,” said Bruce and absentmindedly reaching down to fondle the ears of the dog who by this time was obviously beside herself with love.

Dogs are like that. They can instantly know if they like someone or hate them. However, in this case Greta didn’t like Bruce she plainly adored him. She rolled over and presented her stomach for a rub and her tongue gave him a big lick on his hand.

“Jeez getta load at that it’s about a foot long,” said Bruce looking at the tongue and thinking of all the germs. His other love Spottie, the fox terrier, also was in the habit of breeding colonies of germs on his face at any opportunity with a good licking.

“Ha ha, she has taken a licking not a liking to you Bruce,” laughed Jane while she thought, “hmm so he likes dogs and they like him, that’s a good sign.”

After having a quick chat with her father the two of them escaped the office and went along to the Ladies Lounge for a drink. Bruce had a Blue Bow Pelato orange soda and Jane sipped on a Shandy.

“After we have our drinks why don’t we go on down to the fish shop and buy some hot chips Jane and then we can go on down and sit on the sea wall and look at the surf,” said Bruce hoping that this lovely girl would say yes. This was like his dream at Booleroo and Bruce pinched himself to see if he was awake.

“Sounds good Bruce and Greta would love the walk.”

It was a lovely night by then and the beach was almost deserted. Bruce realised that he and Jane were getting on like a house on fire. For the first time in his life he found that he could talk to a girl without feeling awkward and he rambled on and told her about some of his adventures making sure he sounded heroic.

The three lovers sat there and watched the moon over the waters at Bondi beach

Jane laughed over his tale about being stuck on old Bob the Brumby and not being able to get off.

She giggled over Rancid the Ram and thought that Sally the Sow had a good case for misbehaviour.

"After all it was not her fault that the hairdresser Madam what's her name had some food," laughed Jane.

Sitting there in the balmy evening while the moon started its long journey crawling up the sky was a time which Bruce wanted to last for ever.

"By the way Bruce if you come and work with me at the Pub what can I tell Dad about you. You know what can you do?"

Bruce thought for awhile and realised he did not have too many good points that would be suitable for working in a pub but he had a try anyway.

"I know how to ride a horse, Janie old girl," as he fondled her ears, the Alsatian's that is.

"Yes Bruce, that's nice but what else can you do?"

Bruce thought for awhile and nothing really came into his head but he said, "Shear a sheep and crutchem and ..... "

"Yes Bruce but what else would you know for instance about working in a hotel?"

By now Bruce is getting the drift of the conversation and brightened up after having a brain wave.

"I know a bit about drinking in a pub the lads used to take me along in the truck when we drove into Enngonia. I had a few lemon squashes I don't mind telling you. Jeez it was hot!"

"That's great Bruce that will impress Dad no end," said Jane with a smile.

"How would it be if I asked Dad to find a place for you on the staff and instead of Jackerooing and learning how to be a sheep station manager you can learn to be a manager of a hotel? We could see more of you that way and Greta would like it too I am sure."

"Jeez, Janie old girl that sounds great," murmured Bruce while his heart beat so fast he thought it would tear a hole in his chest.

The next day Bruce phoned Booleroo Station to talk to his mate Whippy.

"Gidday Whippy owareyerz? I am not goin to be coming back to Booleroo mate. Can youse tell the foreman? I may get a job in a hotel down here," shouted Bruce into the phone.

"There is no doubt about you Brucie me boy, I suppose the next thing you tell me is that you have met a publican's daughter and she is sweet on you," came the faint reply from Whippy.

"No doubt about yah Whippy you must be a mind reader how didja know that old mate," laughed Bruce.

"I don't believe it, you haven't met a girl already have you? I warned you to watch out for the sheilas."

"Don't worry Whippy she is a real corker a bonza girl and her Dad owns a pub!"

"Well you have fallen on your feet this time Bruce that's for sure. You really mean you will not be coming back? I will have to tell the boss and all the fellas, they will miss you.

"Yes sorry Whippy it looks like I will get a job down here at the pub and I can train to be a hotel manager."

"The flies will miss yah too Bruce!"

The two friends spoke for awhile longer on the phone knowing that they most probably would never see each other again. Bruce had a real opportunity to make good and he well believed that it would be an easier life at the hotel than being on a sheep station out in the western parts of the state of New South Wales, near Engonnia.

"Well hooroo mate and give my best to the lads, and remember if you are down in Sydney come on over to the pub and see us," said Bruce.

"Yeh cobber I may just do that, hooroo mate," chuckled Whippy as he hung up.

"Jeez, I will be missing the fellows and not the flies," laughed Bruce.

The End

GLOSSARY

To read the Australian way of talking you will note that some Aussies tend to run their words together. For example "Giddayowareyougoin" may sound and read like one word. However, it means a greeting, "Good day how are you going?"

.303 Lee Enfield - This is a British service rifle with a ten shot box magazine with a .303 calibre. Used extensively in the bush and on properties to keep down vermin like, wild pigs, foxes, dingoes and the odd Roo that get's into the wheat or Mrs. Fisher's garden.

.303 round - a bullet

Aborigine, aboriginal, Abo - the indigenous people of Australia. Many of them being employed on the sheep stations as drovers and Jackeroos.

Alsatian - a German Shepherd dog

Amber brew - beer, a cold one, a coldie

Ant's nest - The giant and primitive ants of Australia make a nest in the ground where there is a hole/entrance in the hard ground and a mound of earth up to half a metre in height. If you step on the ant's nest then they come boiling up out of the nest and attack you.

A draw - Where the two people playing a game have an equal score at the end of the match.

Argetorfwillya - oh, get off will you?

Arvo, this arvo - Australian slang for afternoon.

Aussie - someone from Australia as apposed to a Pommie from Britain.

Austin A40 - a sedan motor car made by the British company Austin Motor Company. Forty horsepower of speeding rust.

Bex - a headache remedy

Big uns - big ones

Black fella - an affectionate term for an aboriginal

Blighter - a person, a silly person or an affectionate reference to a friend or acquaintance.

Bludger - someone who will not work or work hard.

Blue Bow - the maker of soft drinks, sodas, for a chain of Hotels at that time.

Bondi beach - the famous beach just south of the city of Sydney.

Bonza, bonzer - Australian for terrific or wonderful.

Booleroo - Boolaroo - an aboriginal name for lone hill, but knowing the aboriginal sense of humour it could be anything.

Boot - known as a trunk. The rear storage area of a car Australian and British.

Bourke - A country town west of Sydney in New South Wales, Australia

Bowl - to throw the ball over-arm to the batsman, a cricket term.

Brekkie - Australian slang for breakfast.

Brumby - a wild horse sometimes domesticated and broken to the saddle. You are a brumby - means you are a loner with little breeding

Brung - bring or brought

Brylcreem - a popular cream for grooming men's hair in the 1950's.

Bunyip - an aboriginal mythical beast, like the Yeti or Bigfoot.

Burlap - hessian bags for wheat and chaff

Cause - because

Chaff bag - a hessian sack

Clip - the shearing of a sheep or the total amount of wool shorn from the mob.

Cobber - pal, friend or a mate.

Condensed Milk - a thick white syrup heavily sweetened

Cooees - a call shouted out by people wishing to be heard over long distances. The Cooee carries a long way.

Corker - English term for a good sort or a good thing.

Corroboree - An Aboriginal ceremony, dancing with music from their culture's instruments.

Coulda - could have

Coz - because

Crows - Australian Raven like birds. A shiny black with a wicked beak and a mournful Ark Arrrrk sound. A carrion feeder and not well liked.

Cricket - a ball game of English origin. The best game in the world.

Crickie - Crikey an exclamation like golly

Cricket match - a game of cricket

Cuppa - Australian slang for a cup of tea.

Dags - the encrustation of dirt and other matter on the hindquarters of a sheep which is caught in the wool.

Dettol - an antiseptic in a bottle

Didja - did you

Dingoes - an Australian wild dog brought to the country by the Aboriginal peoples. It cannot bark. However, it can interbreed with domestic dogs and can be a danger to stock.

Divots - a lump of dirt or dirt and grass hacked out of the ground.

Dog box - this is a term used when describing the type of railway carriage. An apartment of two benches facing each other.

Drenching, crutching etc - This is when the sheep are managed. Drenching when they are herded through a bath of chemicals to kill and parasites. Crutching cleaning a sheep's hindquarters.

Drover - workers employed to look after the sheep, usually on horseback.

Dubbo - a large regional town south of Bourke

Dunt - don't

Ead - head

Enngonia - a small country town near Bourke

Ewe - a female sheep

Eyes peeled - a colloquial term meaning to be very watchful or aware.

Fellas - fellows, chaps, the boys, mates

Feral pigs - domestic pigs that have escaped into the bush and within a few generations have reverted to a wild type with mainly black hair and a longer snout than their domestic cousins. A mob of pigs can be very destructive to crops and also lambs.

Fetlocks - back of a horses leg just above the hoof

Fieldsman - a member of a cricket team. There are two opposing teams to play the game.

Fisser - Fizzer - something that fails to eventuate or a poor effort.

Flag Ale - a well known beer

Full blood - an aboriginal with no mixed ancestry.

Galahs - are pink and grey parrots that fly in large flocks of up to many hundreds. You are a galah - means you are silly. Noisy galah - just imagine a huge flock of parrots arguing away with each other, means you are a noisy person.

Gaol - English and Australian spelling for jail

Gl - a popular cordial when mixed with water and ice cubes it is a refreshing drink in Summer, a bright green colour.

Gidday - a greeting which means Good day.

Giddayowareyerz - good day how are you

Ginger Nut biscuits - round cookies, very hard and sweet flavoured with ginger. The Denist's Friend, made by Arnotts, an Australian company.

Goodonyer - good on you. Well done

Good sort - a person who is good looking or a generally nice person.

Good un - a good one

Gorn - gone

Gunna - going to, going to do something

Hells Bells and Buggy Bells - a colloquial term when someone expresses surprise at an event of some importance.

Hooroo - Australian - see you later, goodbye

Hot chips - French fries

Hot footed - to run fast

House dog - on many cattle or sheep properties (ranches) the house dog is usually a pet and may be anything from a cocker spaniel to a Labrador. As apposed to a working dog which is not a pet or is it petted. It is there to work sheep or cattle and lives rough.

Howareyerz - how are you

Humpies - an aboriginal dwelling made of wood and branches or corrugated iron.

Huntsman's pie - English meal of left over meat baked in a pie or under mashed potato

Hurricane lamp - a glass covered lamp which keeps out the mightiest of winds such as a hurricanes, which would extinguish many other types of lamps.

Jackeroo - ranch hand or drover on a sheep or cattle station, usually young and gaining experience to be a property manager.

Jodhpur - pants or slacks loose in the thigh but tight from the knee down - used for riding.

Kerosene - paraffin - fuel for the lamp.

Lamb - a young sheep

Lamingtons - Australia's National Dish. Just joking. Consisting of squares of sponge cake dipped in chocolate sauce and then rolled in crumbed cocoanut.

Lemonade - was easily purchased in Australia at this time. It was a clear tart, sweet drink tasting of lemons. Cola drinks like Coca Cola were not easily available at this time.

Lemon squash - a cloudy yellow soft and sweet drink tasting of lemons.

Life saver - a trained lifeguard stationed on a beach to aid surfers or swimmers in trouble.

Lignum - a shrub or small tree growing in bushes no higher than say 2 or 3 metres, covering the ground for huge areas. The wild pigs live in these areas and also the wildlife and sheep or cattle. Usually growing in dry country.

Locomotive - a train

Mob or mob of sheep - an Australian term for a herd of sheep.

Nyngan - a small country town on the Mitchell Highway to Bourke

Orf - off

OP Rum - Overproof red rum. A strong alcoholic drink made by Bundaberg. The Cockie's Medicine and keeps you warm in winter.

Outback - the back country of the State of New South Wales. In the most case semi desert and way out the back of beyond.

Owareya - how are you

Owaryerz - how are you

Paddock - Australian term for a piece of ground of considerable size, usually casually fenced.

Party Line - the old telephone system where the call had to be placed through a manual telephone exchange operator and the line was used by all the people in the vicinity. You could therefore, hear other people's conversations.

Pelato - a carbonated orange juice, a soda, made by Blue Bow.

Peters Ice Cream - a popular brand of ice cream at that time. Vanilla being Bruce's favourite.

Plod - An English term for a policeman sometimes used in Australia along with Copper, Cop or walloper.

Pikelets - a small type of sweet pancake, English.

Pin up - a photograph in the Pix magazine of a young woman usually dressed in a bathing suit or swimming costume.

Pitch - The centre of the sports ground or oval where a cricket match is played. The Pitch is an area between the creases.

Pix magazine - a popular magazine in Australia during the 1950's.

Pommie - someone who came from Britain. Usually an affectionate swipe at a Brit.

Pub - a hotel where there is all manner of alcohol drinks are served, beer being preferred in summer because of the weather. Usually men only at this time in Australia woman could have a drink in the Ladies Lounge or sit in the car outside.

Public bar - the place in the hotel where the men drink their beer or spirits.

Pulling your leg - fooling you or making fun of you a practical joke

Rabbits - these animals were a huge problem at this time in Australia. They were introduced to the country and bred in great numbers due to no natural predators.

Read sign - the Aboriginal trackers are experts at following tracks of animals and the like and can therefore read the signs of the animals passing.

Ram - a male sheep

Roos - Kangaroos the Australian marsupial. Hops along with their big tail behind as balance. The females are called Does, the males Bucks and the babies are Joeys.

Rotten flies - In sheep country in Australia the problem of swarms of flies is always evident. They seek out any moisture in this dry country and eyes, areas of perspiration and the like are sometimes black with them.

Roustabout - a man employed on a property who can do just about all the chores or jobs required. A handy man to have around.

Scarpered - English expression for running away or escaping.

Scrub - Australian term for an area of country covered by small trees and shrubs.

Shandy - a long drink of a mix of beer and lemonade.

Sheep duffers - Australian colloquial term for rustlers or sheep stealers.

Shearers quarters - on the sheep property there is usually a building available to them for their living quarters for the shearers and the drovers.

Sheep station - an Australian ranch or property stocking sheep for wool.

Sheila - young woman.

Shillings - the Australian currency before conversion to dollars was pounds, shillings and pence. One shilling is equivalent to ten cents.

Shot through - run away

Shoulda - should have

Smart Aleck - a person who is a know all but knows nothing.

SP bookie - an illegal bookmaker taking bets for horse, trotters and dog races.

Stock horse - Australian; a horse trained to work with cattle or sheep.

Stock whip - made out of plaited hide, it has a handle of hard plaited leather which continues into the whip's body proper. It has at the end a slim piece of cord or leather. When swung the correct way it can hurt. It makes a loud crack sound. The sound hurries or guides for example the cattle. The cracking sound can also move the mob of sheep along.

Tank - a bush term for an earthen dam. Usually scraped out of the ground - a place for the animals to drink. Both herds of sheep and cattle frequent the dam and compete with Kangaroos, wild pigs and many more animals.

This arvo - this afternoon

Tie a line - affix a rope to something

Tooheys KB - A popular brand of beer served cold in Australia.

Torch - flashlight, a light powered by a battery.

Top paddock - an expanse of land in the northern direction from the homestead

Trangie - a small country town west of Sydney on the Mitchell Highway to Bourke

Tribesman - usually an aboriginal belonging to one of the local tribes

Trimmings - in an Australian roast dinner, this usually consists of roast lamb, roast potatoes, rpumpkin, and gravy with mint sauce. Very English.

Tucker - food, Australian derived from one of the Aboriginal dialects.

Two piece swimming costume - the forerunner of a bikini.

Utility Truck - Ute - a sedan able to seat only 3 people on a bench seat with a tray on the back

Vincents APC - a headache remedy in powder form.

Wags - jokers

Whacked - hit, punched

Whacko the Diddlyoh - a colloquial term for saying something is great or wonderful

White fella - the aboriginals sometimes refer to people of European descent as white (fellows) fellas. In the 1950's no body really expressed any argument with this type of racial stereotyping.

Whingin' - whinging, complaining

Wild dogs - the Australian wild dog is usually the Dingo brought to the continent by the aboriginal people. However, many domestic dogs go wild and breed with dingoes and hunt in packs. They can cause considerable damage to the wild life and sheep.

Wivout - without

Womans Weekly - a very popular magazine for ladies.

Working dog - is not a pet or is it petted. It is there to work sheep or cattle and lives rough. They are usually Kelpie, or Boarder Collie crosses with Blue Cattle dogs popular in some areas also. These are different to the house dogs which on many cattle or sheep properties (ranches) is a pet and lives a life of relative ease.

Walkabout - the aboriginal people long being nomadic enjoy moving from one place to another. It is also a spiritual journey where they are at one with the land as they walk along.

Woulda - would have

Yah - you

Yairz - yes with a drawl in the voice

Yarn - a story, a good yarn is a good story.

Yarning - just talking.

Yer - you

Yer - your

Yerz - you

You are a brumby - means you are a loner with little breeding

Youse - you

More Jackeroo

You can follow Bruce and his mates on their adventures in a new book.

You can buy the books at all good bookstores or from Amazon

Other books written and Illustrated by

Steve McGregor

THE ADVENTURES OF WALLY

Suitable for children 6 years of age onwards

A young Aboriginal boy called Wally living in the country area of Australia.

Ideal for children and also young adults living in Australia or overseas. These delightful books are an introduction to how the original people of Australia may have lived only a short time ago.

There are five books in the series:

Wally and the Boomerang

Wally the Warrior

Wally and the Hunt for the Giant Bunyip

Wally Goes Fishing

Wally and the Poachers

Introducing Wally...

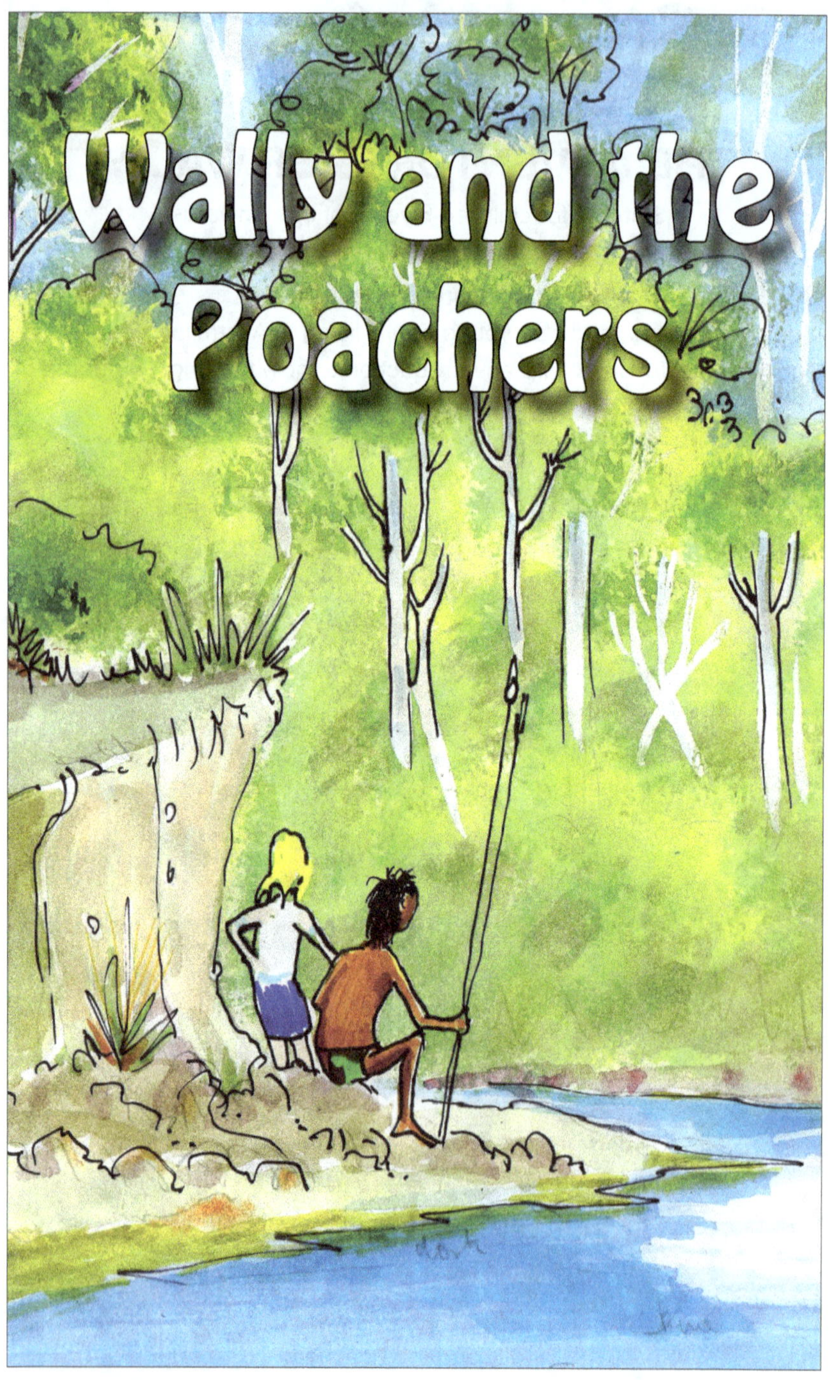

Wally was just hanging around the camp one day watching his mother grinding some seeds to make flour when he looked up to see the local Ranger with a girl beside him, walking towards them.

The Park Ranger who then introduced his young daughter, Skye, to them and asked if there was someone from the tribe who could come and help him study the local wildlife.

Wally quickly asked his Mother if it would be alright for him to help the Ranger, and with a nod of her head he rushed to get his spears,

boomerang and gear. In no time he was ready.

"What is that?" said Skye.

"Oh, it's just a lizard called a goanna but this is only a little fellow and should do the family for lunch," laughed Wally with a big grin on his face.

"Ooh er, I hope you cook it first,' said Skye

The two children soon became friends and Skye wanted to have a close look at Wally's spear so he handed it over to her so she could see what it was like close up.

"The spear maker in my tribe made it for me and I practice as much as I can so when I become a warrior I will be able to hunt for tucker." Said Wally.

Eventually Wally and Skye arrived at the camp and the Ranger, who had also returned said. "I have to drive into town to buy some supplies at the store and as it is quite a distance I will not be back 'till morning. "

Skye asked him, "Daddy can I stay with Wally in the camp we want to go and have a swim."

Later when they were both standing in the shallow water of the billabong Wally showed Skye a fish he caught.

After they finished their swim they dried themselves and Skye said, “Oh Wally this morning Daddy and I saw some strange men camped down the creek. Why don’t we go and see what they are up to?”

To find out what happens next to Wally and Skye you can buy the books at www.stephenmcgregorartist.com.au or on Amazon.com.au

HERE'S EDDIE MULLIGAN

In the 1950's Australia was a different place for children compared to the decade starting 2010.

There was no television, few cars and mechanical implements to make ones life easier. Children had to find their own entertainment, horse riding, walking in the bush, riding a Billy cart or ones bicycle were just some of the simple pleasures for a boy like Eddie.

His mate Piggy Andrews was a lot different to Eddie although they were great friends. Piggy was more studious and serious. However, the boys had wonderful adventures and times together.

There are two books in the series:

The Adventures of Eddie Mulligan

It's hard being Eddie Mulligan

Introducing Eddie...

Chapter 1 - The lady with the moustache

Eddie Mulligan was always looking for a bit of excitement, but going out with Mum and Dad was not always something he enjoyed.

Eddie looked at the lady and his mouth dropped open

Eddie was showing signs of a becoming a joker and was at that stage where he would come out with the funniest of sayings; well at least his proud parents thought so! His Dad, Big Pat, was a typical Irishman, red cheeked with a shock of black hair and the bluest of eyes that God created. He would often say with a big smile and in the brogue that he still retained, "Ah me Eddie is a good Boyo and just like meself at that age."

It was only a few weeks previously when the family were having a meal at the local Chinese café that Eddie tucking into his chicken chow mien was asked by the waitress who spoke in a strong accented voice, "You like?"

Quick as a flash Eddie replied with a beaming smile, "You must be the Old Lady from Bali Hai, you know from the filum South Pacific."

The waitress just looked vacant and drifted off back to the kitchen while Eddie's family all put their heads down and concentrated on their meal. They were getting used to Eddie's clever asides.

If you listened really closely though you would have heard Mum say to Big Pat with a heavy sigh, "It's all too much sometimes."

For a time there was nothing to be heard but a steady munching from the Mulligan family. Eventually though the silence must have got to Eddie for he brightened up perceptibly as his Dad said, "Now Eddie how are you getting along at school with your reading lessons. Can you read yet?

To which Eddie replied, "Yeh."

"Can you read backwards?"

"Yeh"

"Can you read upside down?"

"Er, yeh"

His Dad, speaking French, "Can you speak French"?

"Er, no ... but I can speak Korean, just like me mate Lionel, he's from Korea and he has taught me a lot" said Eddie with a silly look on his face.

"Good, well say something in Korean."

He then said something in Korean

"What does that mean?" his Mum said with a glimmer of interest.

"Shit head"

"Golly!" said Pat

"Eddie, Eddie Mulligan," shouted his Mum in horror.

Some days after the interesting meal at the Chinese café the Mulligan family were told by Dad that they would be going on an excursion.

"Where to Dad?" said Eddie with his piping boy's voice.

"We will be going to the local plant nursery Eddie and you will be able to see all the flowers and shrubs," said Eddie's Mum with a smile.

"Aw, Mum that sounds real dopey, can't I stay at home and go and see me mate Piggy?" moaned Eddie.

"No Eddie it is my mate," Eddie's Dad corrected.

"Piggy's not your mate Dad, he's me mate," replied our favourite hero while scratching his head in surprise.

The family piled into the family car and off they went.

Already Eddie was bored as he sat in the back looking at his bare feet. Already the journey seemed to have gone on for such a long time that at last Eddie piped up.

A voice was then heard from the back seat. "Are we there yet Dad?"

His ever suffering parents did not even bother to turn around and just hunched their heads into their shoulders and hoped that young Eddie would soon get used to the drive and look out the window or something.

When they arrived at their destination the place was everything that they expected.

"It is lovely and spring has surely arrived; just look at the flowers of all sizes and colours, Eddie."

Eddie just concentrated on looking at the little red haired girl who just happened to be innocently walking past. He stuck his tongue out at her and pulled an ugly face and the poor girl recoiled and turned to the adult with her and said, "Oh, Mummy that horrid boy was ever so rude to me."

Eddie smiled in delight and looked around for his next victim.

Eddie's parents trudged on and walked slowly up and down the paths and let young Eddie wander a little while keeping an eye on him to make sure he did not stray or upset any other little girl.

Pat and Mum were side by side and just sauntering along when they noticed an odd sight.

Coming down the path towards them was a middle aged woman. She was normal in every way except for one thing; she was sporting a dark brown, almost black moustache, and was one of those women who would not, for some weird reason, shave the thing off.

Now this moustache was not a dusting of fine hairs on her upper lip but a bristling bushy affair stuck under her nose.

Pat knew that his boy, their big mouthed commentator on life's misfortunes and jokes, would say something about the hairy member of the human race coming closer at each ominous step.

He and his darling wife both knew instinctively that Eddie was too far away to grab him and put a hand over his mouth or grip him tightly by the neck.

So without a word spoken Eddie's Mum went right and Pat swerved left down each path to hide before they were embarrassed by their tactless little hero.

It was when we were both hidden in the colourful undergrowth that they heard the loud piping voice of their dear child.

"Mum, Dad lookit the lady wiv a moustache!" as Eddie chortled, shaking with laughter.

In no time the woman had gone on her way, hopefully never to appear in their life again. Silently Pat and Mum met back on the main path and collected Eddie tightly by his hand and agreed to go somewhere else, in fact anywhere else just to have some peace.

In the drive home Eddie's parents marvelled at their successful tactics to escape an embarrassing moment and his Mum weakly said, "Do you think that we will have any more of those times before he is off our hands?"

Eddie's bowed and beaten father Pat gripped the steering wheel tighter and rolled his eyes heavenward and quietly vowed, "I will just have to be even more on the lookout than before and promise meself that I will never be caught again."

Alas his feeble prayer was not answered as he was to find out for many years to come.

Eddie's Dad from that day forth never once said, "That boy of mine that Eddie, ha ha ha is a chip off the old block."

Though what he did say and say very quietly so Mum would not hear, as he scratched his head, "That Eddie, I don't know who he is but he must take after his Mother's side of the family."

ABOUT THE AUTHOR

Writing this book may well show that I am a better cartoonist than a story teller. Anyhow the saga of Bruce from Bondi a Jackeroo in the 1950's gave me a laugh. I suspect that I have struck a chord here with my own outlook on city and country life. The hapless gormless youth of Bruce the Jackeroo shows that not all of us are born with brains or able to be smooth and accomplish great things. Bruce is a fish out of water, a city boy struggling to be a man in the Australian countryside of the 1950's when it was still pretty rough. He does however, come good and matures.

The two Eddie Mulligan tales that are also in this book are however, a little different because younger audiences may enjoy them. Eddie is a youngster in the 1950's and there is not a lot to do. However, Eddie and his best mate Piggy Andrews make their own fun and some of their many adventures grace the pages of these books.

Now with the illustrations you might like to know I studied Commercial Art at East Sydney technical College in the early 1960's and also tried my hand later at oil painting and watercolours. My style is a simple yet expressive one characterised by bright washes of water colour and black ink outlines.

Basically I try to keep it simple and avoid fiddling. The effect is what I am after and as long as I get close and try and ignore all the technical bloops then I will stop at that.

Now have a read about our young heroes and I hope you have a lot of fun.

Steve McGregor, 2013

Contact : Stevemcgregor3@bigpond.com

Website: www.stephenmcgregorartist.com.au

www.ingramcontent.com/pod-product-compliance
Lightning Source LLC
Chambersburg PA
CBHW070622120726
47909CB00004B/1280